A BURNING INFERNO

At the last instant the nose of the helicopter came up, but it was still traveling too fast when it struck the road. There were loud reports as the tires burst, then the undercarriage was ripped off. The chopper's broadside progress across the intersection was accompanied by the scream of grinding metal on stone and billowing clouds of sparks and smoke, through which scythed lengths of splintered blade and shattered panes of glass.

With a final jarring collision the cabin came to rest, and as it did the unchecked racing howl of the twin turboshaft engines died. The silence was short-lived. Even as Libby's sound-saturated eardrums began to recognize the fact that they had stopped, their deafening racket was replaced by another that played on a wider range of nerves. A hideous, nerve-shredding, distressed howling began to emanate from the cockpit.

"*Out.* It's starting to burn."

The hefty shove Hyde gave him in the back helped Libby shake some of the shock from his mind, and he leapt down from the doorway to start helping out the others. A fierce fire raged over their heads as the flames fed on the punctured tanks of aviation fuel. Every breath was filled with the stench of kerosene and burning rubber . . .

THE SURVIVALIST SERIES
by Jerry Ahern

SKY STRIKE

By James Rouch

ZEBRA BOOKS
KENSINGTON PUBLISHING CORP.

ZEBRA BOOKS

are published by

Kensington Publishing Corp.
475 Park Avenue South
New York, NY 10016

First Zebra Books printing: February 1986

Printed in the United States of America

For Carola Edmond,
who guided me through the Second World War,
and Nick Webb, who led me into the Third

. . . and in conclusion . . . this committee recognizing that the battlefield of the future will be dominated by the guided missile . . . it is recommended that the production of manned combat aircraft be stopped as soon as is possible under the terms of existing contracts . . . and that all new projects, at whatever stage of development, be cancelled immediately.

The above is taken from the last page of a consultative document, one of several, considered prior to the final drafting of the British Government's Defence White Paper published in April 1957, that declared manned combat aircraft to be obsolete.

This document was circulated among senior Air Ministry Staff, who were invited to append their comments. On this particular copy, now in private hands, the only note, pencilled alongside the conclusion in the margin, and alleged to be in the handwriting of an air commodore, is "balls."

At the outbreak of World War III, taking the Warsaw Pact and NATO totals together, there were more than 5,300 manned combat aircraft in Central Europe, with over 9,000 in reserve and second-line units, with the Warsaw Pact outnumbering NATO by more than two-to-one.

ONE

She was struggling, trying to push him off, but he wasn't going to stop, not now. Christ it was hurting, the fastener of his zip was biting into the base of his iron-hard erection and the lace trimming on her knickers was like sandpaper against its sensitive tip.

"Can't you wait? At least let me get them down . . . this is no good for me . . . you're making me wet . . ."

He had to finish, had to; he'd waited so long and now, as he'd been afraid it would, it was proving difficult. "Just keep still." His face was in her hair and his every laboured breath was saturated with the blended scents of perfume, deodorant and hair lacquer.

There wasn't enough room on the back seat of the Opel, he could only thrust an inch or so at a time, or his feet became entangled in the door pull or ashtray. It hurt, he'd be sore for days, but he had to finish.

Managing to push forward a fraction, he felt his penis slide on the silk-like material to the shallow smooth valley between her thigh and crotch. Suddenly he knew he could do it, could feel his body priming itself as he rubbed harder and harder and faster and faster. Now, it had to be now . . . now . . .

"I don't like this, let me . . . oh you sod, you dirty sod. You've done it all over me, it's running down my leg. Get up, get off me. No, stop, you're dragging my dress through it . . . have you got a tissue . . . ? be quick. You rotten sod, what a mess . . . it's all between my legs . . ."

Somehow Libby half-turned, opened the car door and backed out. Before he walked away he threw her his handkerchief. He didn't want to, but he saw her, by the pale illumination of the interior light. She'd pulled herself to a slumped position against the far door and was holding up her skirt and parting her legs. Grabbing the folded white linen she shook it out, bunched it and wiped the slow white avalanche from the hem of her underwear, and from among the stray strands of pubic hair escaping beneath it.

Well, he'd done it, and he hated himself for it. Not because of her, she'd been keen enough to leave the Naafi and go off with him, not because of the discomfort he experienced as he tucked his fast-shrinking self back into his clothes, there'd been several times in the last couple of years when he'd made it that bad himself by exercising it: no, he hated himself for having done it at all. He'd betrayed Helga, broken the impossible promise he'd made to himself when he'd heard she was among the millions of civilians trapped by the Russian advance.

He didn't look around when he heard the door

slam, or when he heard her approaching. A small fist half-heartedly punched him on the arm.

"That wasn't fair, not after getting me going. Are you going to have a proper go? I don't mind, if you let me get ready this time."

"No, no, I don't want anything else . . . I'm sorry, I can't explain, I just needed it that way, just once." So the Zone hadn't made him totally sub-human, yet. There was still some decency in him if he could summon up an apology of sorts for an easy pick-up like her. "Look, I'll make it up to you, give you some money for some new things if you like."

"Alright, I'll let you, seeing as how that's the least you can do. You must have stained them, you did a load, it went everywhere, I've never seen so much. What are you looking at?"

From the high ground, southern Germany stretched away into the night, marked randomly but liberally by the lights of farms and villages, and occasionally gashed by the beams from vehicle headlamps. But far short of the invisible horizon the sprinkling of white and yellow pinpoints ended abruptly, as though a black sheet had been draped over the landscape beyond.

"That's the Zone isn't it? I don't like being this close, gives me the shudders."

Libby resisted the urge to push her off when she wrapped her arms about him. "Yes, that's the Zone."

In the far distance a star shell burst and made a bright oasis for perhaps thirty seconds as the parachute-suspended fiery ball of magnesium drifted to the ground.

"Are you going back in there?"

"Yes, soon."

"Is it as bad as they say? Do you have to go?"

"It's worse actually, far worse, but I don't have to go, I want to go, want to." Now he felt her move away, as though she were suddenly afraid of him. Perhaps, perhaps he was no longer human after all.

TO: HEADQUARTERS—GROUP OF SOVIET
     FORCES GERMANY—ZOSSEN-WUNSDORF
FOR: THE SPECIAL ATTENTION OF
     LIEUTENANT GENERAL ALEKSEEV
     DEPUTY COMMANDER—AIR DEFENCE—
     EASTERN EUROPE
FROM: GENERAL PAKOVSKI—OFFICER
     COMMANDING AIR DEFENCE
     REGIMENTS—CENTRAL SECTOR—ZONE

Transmission. Priority. By Special General Staff Code AP/43.
Secure link or hand only

Comrade Lieutenant General

Acting on Intelligence information passed by your office and following orders issued by yourself the action listed below has been carried out:

1. The 867th (reinforced) light anti-aircraft battalion: the 12th anti-aircraft missile regiment: the 727th armoured medium anti-aircraft regiment: have been moved to cover the rail junction and marshalling yards at Kothen.

2. All movements have been made by night under conditions of strict radio silence. Counter-intelligence measures have been taken to prevent the enemy detecting the redeployment.

3. All battery commanders have been ordered not to activate their radar systems until the destruction of our light screen of radar pickets signals the imminent

approach of the expected NATO attack. Under these conditions our main defences will survive to engage the enemy force at close range, when their destruction will be assured.

As required, I can give the Comrade Lieutenant General my personal assurance that not a single capitalist mercenary will survive the implementation of this plan. I am moving my own HQ to a site near Kothen to maintain the closest possible supervision.

Signed: GENERAL PAKOVSKI

TWO

Libby kept a tight grip on the mini-gun, as the slipstream buffeted the heavy cluster of barrels projecting through the open cabin door of the helicopter.

The eastern fringes of the Zone were below them now, an ugly land, banded by swathes of chemically stunted sickly vegetation. A whole forest lay flattened, the stripped and charred trunks laid in patterns that marked the paths of massive blast waves from a nuclear bomb or missile burst.

Among the clumps of yellow foliage Libby could see occasional patches of green, where some hardy plant was using the new strength of spring to restart its battle for survival.

There were no targets for the snaking belt of mixed armour-piercing and tracer rounds. They had been told at the briefing there wouldn't be, but he was disappointed all the same.

He leant out, and damp air rushing past pushed against his visor and sucked the air from beneath it, so he had to gasp for breath. Visibility was improving fast as the sun rose higher. When he looked back he could see the second wave of the assault, five miles behind them and stretching away to north and south, bank after bank of Black Hawks and Chinooks, many with underslung loads.

A Soviet scout car swerved from the track along which it had been making its lonely patrol as the choppers swept overhead, at a hundred feet their massed rotors sending the plants and puddles into wild waving motion.

It was gone before he could sight on it, but he gripped the multi-barrelled gun tighter, in expectation of other opportunities soon.

Now they crossed the rusting wire and overgrown mine-fields of the old Iron Curtain, and then they were over East Germany and the helicopter sank to fifty feet as it raced above the ill-kept fields and dilapidated villages, following every contour of the rolling land.

"Will you look at this?" Ripper rubbed the fabric of his camouflage top between a filthy thumb and forefinger. "This is all brand new, it's just like we were going to a party."

"Command must have heard we were having trouble getting you to wash, so they figured the only way to get you clean was to change your nappy." Digging Andrea in the ribs with his elbow, Dooley waited for the laugh he considered his due. It didn't come.

"Twenty minutes to the DZ. Check your weapons." Revell came back into the cabin from the cockpit. He carried his new 12-gauge assault rifle

16

cradled in his arms. Four of the big drum magazines hung from his tight-hitched belt. Standing with his legs apart, he needed no hand-hold to counter the motion of the Black Hawk as it maintained maximum speed.

A burst of rapid automatic fire was audible from the next chopper in line. Libby couldn't see the other door gunner's target, but watched the arc of tracer spiral down to a farmyard. Smoke and a bubble of red flame were rising above the roofs as it was lost to view.

Bombardier Cline was finding it difficult to stay on the seat he had improvised from a stack of spare flak-jackets, teetering back and forth at every slight turbulence.

"Frightened of losing something, Bomber?"

Pretending not to hear, Cline ignored Dooley. The big oaf was just letting off steam, no point in getting involved in a slanging match with him. Not only could he not be certain of winning, it would look bad in front of the Yank officer.

Noise and vibration rippled through the hull as the minigun unleashed fifty rounds. Sergeant Hyde moved to the door and looked out past their gunner. A fast settling plume of mud and debris partly obscured a sandbag-protected light flak-cannon. There was hardly time for it to register before it was gone.

It wasn't possible for Hyde to tell if the weapon had been hit and damaged, probably it had, judging by the amount of muck that had been thrown up around it, but one thing was certain, it had been unmanned. His shouted warning to conserve ammunition was drowned by the roar of jets as a pair of A10 Thunderbolts, from the squadrons assigned to fly Wild Weasel flak, SAM and radar suppression missions, zipped past, deposited their entire load of externally carried stores on a seemingly innocuous stretch of woodland, and pulled sharply up and away into the sun.

Eyes watering, Libby watched the parachute-retarded fall of the cluster and fragmentation bombs. Just above the tree tops, each disintegrated: the cluster munitions into their hundreds of deadly and variously delayed bomblets and the daisy cutters into their millions of razor-sharp fragments.

"They said we wouldn't see much opposition. Looks like the airforce is determined to reduce that to none at all." Through the smoke Hyde could discern the hulls of several tracked SAM missile launchers, a whole battery. Some were partially buried by the trunks and foliage that had been intended to merely conceal them. More trees were falling, toppling across trucks and trailers already damaged by blast and fragments. Several spreadeagled bodies were fleetingly visible.

As the scene of the devastation was left behind they flew over a collection of a dozen Zil and Tatra trucks, all of them burning fiercely. Flames rose high, to lick about the radar dishes and masts on their roofs.

"Looks like our flyers poked out the Commies' eyes before coming back to hit the hardware." Libby saw the handful of troops attempting to tackle the fire throw away their extinguishers and run as the chopper squadrons beat past overhead.

Now, save for where it persisted in a few scattered

hollows, the mist had dispersed.

"Kothen in ten minutes. If Intelligence has got it right, we're through the main anti-aircraft defences. From here on in it'll just be random light stuff." Revell declined the mint Ripper was offering. "No, thanks. I've seen the effect they have on others."

Only Clarence accepted, pausing from checking the ammunition clips for his Enfield Enforcer sniper rifle to take two. He put both in his mouth at once and chewed vigorously without change of expression, to Ripper's obvious disappointment.

Twice they passed over military convoys and both times Libby made ready to return fire, but there was none. It might be different for the second wave. Several transporters and field cars sported pintle-mounted heavy machine guns.

Hardly any civilian traffic was to be seen, apart from the occasional tractor or cart-towing pushbike.

A few handfuls of livestock stampeded at the helicopters' approach, running into fences and streams in their panic. For a moment Libby was tempted to put a burst into a scattering herd of cattle, but held back. Hyde was still close by, and the sergeant came down hard on needless expenditure of ammunition, very hard.

Including the belt already in the mini-gun, Libby knew they had six thousand rounds of ammunition for the weapon, less the few he'd fired off. Sounding a lot, in fact at maximum rate of fire, which the gun was quite capable of sustaining, it was just sufficient for one minute of action. But at this rate he'd be taking most of them back.

Movement in a far corner of a large field caught his

eye. Yes, there it was. A rapidly rotating dish topped a tracked armoured hull, and Libby could see a figure, a man, running fast towards it. Other door gunners had seen the target and several lines of tracer hosed towards the vehicle.

One of the blasts of steel and fire cut across the runner; it could only have been by accident, he wasn't worth the expenditure of a tenth of the ammunition. His remains were scattered over the meadow like pink chaff as his torso was nearly slashed into quarters.

For a fraction of time three other streams of bullets converged and pieces flew from the radar carrier also, as it was pounded and half-hidden by the smoke and sparks of the multiple impacts.

There were more buildings below them now. The villages had given way to ribbon development. Revell noted the change and took his seat on the bench, wedging himself between Clarence and Andrea.

The sniper attempted to distance himself from the contact, but there was not enough room on the bench. Instead he closed his eyes and part of his mind to try to ignore it.

Dooley sat chewing his lip, but it wasn't fear that made him distort his stubble-darkened features, or play constantly with the sheathed bayonet at his belt. It was tension, an overpowering surge of adrenalin that would build and build until, at the moment they jumped from the chopper and into action, it would peak and he'd pour his pent-up energies into the battle.

One other person among them exhibited outward

signs of his emotions. Boris was sweating. The Russian deserter frequently had to dab at his face with his cuff to wipe away the beads of moisture that formed faster than the cold draught from the open door could evaporate them. He had not said a word to anyone since the final briefing, when they'd learnt their objective, and now the terrors that churned inside him were draining him of colour.

Leaning forward, Revell tapped the Russian on the knee to get his attention. "We'll be down soon. I'm not all that keen on flying myself."

Shaking his head, Boris stumbled over words he could normally select and speak with impeccable fluency. "It is not . . . not the flying . . ." The major's words sunk in, belatedly, and he hastily corrected himself, grasping at the excuse offered. This time the words came out in a jumbled torrent. "Yes . . . yes it is . . . the flying. I will feel better . . . yes better, when we are down. We will be down . . . soon." That last word came very quietly, was lost in the scream of the engines and the beating whirr of the rotor blades. His face fell, like a man who has just announced his own execution. He had to wipe the sweat away again.

Ahead Libby could see the shining silver parallel strips of railway tracks. They crossed one set, then another, and now they were over a built-up area.

The pilot banked them to a new heading and they began the final approach to the drop zone, having to gain height as they did so, to be sure of clearing power lines, chimneys and radio masts.

A scorching wave of compressed air shoved Libby back into the cabin and he had to grab hold of the mini-gun to keep from falling as the helicopter alongside, that had kept them company for so many miles, dissolved inside a huge orange ball of flame as it was hit by a SAM missile.

Only the blazing hulk of the cabin, with one engine still attached, struck the ground as a recognizable piece of debris. The rest of the Black Hawk and its crew fell as a burning rain on to a waterlogged football pitch.

Further along the line another of their number was hit and began to fall, trailing a sheet of flame. Just before it exploded against the base of a giant cooling tower, Libby saw its door gunner jump. On fire from head to foot, he landed close by a line of tracked missile launchers. A dashing field car deliberately swerved to run over the body.

Their pilot was throwing their transport about the sky, at the same time dropping a series of flares, in an attempt to decoy missiles homing by infra-red.

The evasive tactics were giving Libby little chance to use the mini-gun to effect. He managed to put most of a hundred-round burst across the hull front of a quad-barrelled Shilka flak-tank, but had no chance to see what result he achieved.

Another helicopter cut in front of them, and as it did Libby could clearly see the pilot desperately wrestling with the controls, and the terrified expression of a young door gunner; then there were more targets before him, and he wasn't able to see what sort of landing it made.

Successive curtains of anti-aircraft gunfire sent shells and machine gun calibre bullets smacking into and bouncing off the underside of the reinforced floor. More passed through the arc of the blades, making strange shrieking, zinging noises as they nicked or flattened themselves against the armour rotors.

A lone F-4 appeared from nowhere and unleashed a hail of rockets against a battery of SA-6 missiles and their radars, parked in a railway goods yard alongside a row of four cooling towers. The whole lot blew apart and the fighter-bomber flew through the smoke of their destruction then climbed and turned for a second run across the front of the depleted line of helicopters.

This time the aircraft used its 20mm gatling cannon to lash a group of gun pits, before dropping a pair of iron bombs that straddled a line of parked trucks loaded with spare missiles. Two of them were tipped over, and another began to burn.

Constant vibration made Libby's hands tingle as he sent burst after burst at the never-ending series of anti-aircraft positions.

Another Black Hawk plunged to earth, exploding on impact and giving its crew and passengers no chance of escape.

Tracer of every hue zipped past the cabin door, a large green one passing so close that Libby felt he could have put his hand out and touched it. Bullets beat against the chopper's armoured underside, and ricocheted from its fuselage, making long scars in its camouflage paint scheme.

One mile to go. Libby heard it over his headphones, sandwiched between the constant list of targets the flight crew were feeding him. Not that he had time to search for those the pilots saw, nor did he need to. It seemed that every open space they flew across held its quota of SAM launchers or anti-aircraft guns. It was a concentration of defences the like of which he had never seen before.

A loud bang filled the cabin with deafening noise. Suddenly it was full of smoke and every panel in the fuselage began to shudder violently. Loose fittings bounced and tumbled about the cabin floor, some finding their way out through the doorway. Cline and his stack of bulletproof vests went different ways. Fumes from the engine's automatic fire-suppression system flooded down into the cabin through rents in the plates.

The helicopter was yawing from side to side and losing height. An apartment block flashed past on one side, an electricity pylon on the other.

With the shaking becoming still more violent, Revell was forced to hang on to a bracket with one hand, while the other he stretched out to Andrea.

She had lost her grip and was sliding towards the open door. Twisting round she managed to grasp his extended hand, and as she did Dooley also managed to reach her, and between them they hauled her to safety.

Buildings blurred past Libby as he kept his finger hard down to fire off every round he could before they crashed. There was no aiming, no distinction between military and civilian targets. All he wanted to do was hand out to them, all of them, everything he could, before they got him. They were down very low now, and still with a lot of forward momentum. There was a fire somewhere above his head. An engine, or perhaps a fuel line, was burning, and blow-torchlike feathers of yellow flames kept dipping in through the top of the door to lick at his helmet and visor.

Out of control the Black Hawk side-slipped, the rotors sliced across the front of an office building and the ground raced towards them.

THREE

At the last instant the nose of the helicopter came up, but it was still travelling too fast when it struck the road. There were loud reports as the tyres burst, then the undercarriage was ripped off. The chopper's broadside progress across the intersection was accompanied by the scream of grinding metal on stone and billowing clouds of sparks and smoke, through which scythed lengths of splintered blade and shattered panes of glass.

With a final jarring collision the cabin came to rest, and as it did the unchecked racing howl of the twin turboshaft engines died. The silence was short-lived. Even as Libby's sound-saturated eardrums began to recognise the fact that they had stopped, their deafening racket was replaced by another that played on a wider range of nerves. A hideous, nerve-shredding, distressed howling began to emanate from the cockpit.

"Out. It's starting to burn."

The hefty shove Hyde gave him in the back helped

Libby shake some of the shock from his mind, and he leapt down from the doorway to start helping out the others. A fierce fire raged over their heads as the flames fed on the punctured tanks of aviation fuel. Every breath was filled with the stench of kerosene and burning rubber.

Ripper and Clarence joined Libby in trying to salvage some of the demolition charges. Roasting smoke filled the cabin, and molten aluminum was dripping from the flames overhead.

Attempts to free the trapped co-pilot were hopeless. The concrete lamp standard that had crushed the other flight deck crew had wrapped the metalwork of the cockpit tight around his legs. But it wasn't that pain that prompted the man's ghastly yelling; slashed by scalpel-sharp slivers of glass, the flesh and muscle of his face hung down into the torn hands he cupped to hold them. Like bloody steaks, the flaps of tissue flopped back and forth at his every move.

Taking the kit Revell pushed into his hand, Hyde extracted the syringe, and with the force of a knife-thrust plunged the long thick needle in through a tear in the co-pilot's tattered flak-jacket as close to the heart as he could get, and rammed the plunger home.

As though it mattered against the other agonies and fears he was experiencing, the man jumped and mewed at the sliver of metal's penetration, then the huge overdose hit him and every fibre of his suffering-wracked body relaxed and he died.

Another helicopter passed overhead. Others could be heard, and so could the rattle and crash of automatic and cannon fire. Even as they had been going down, Revell's mind had been interpreting the wild flitting images he'd glimpsed through the cabin windows. The rail junction and marshalling yard could only be a few hundred yards off. Maybe the raid wasn't as big a shambles as it had looked from the air, maybe most of the first wave had got through, and even if they hadn't, the second was due soon; and then they'd have enough men on the ground to do the job and still hold a perimeter against the time when pick-up would be possible.

A decrepit Tatra truck rattled around a corner two blocks away, and several half-dressed East German Militia snapped off a wild fusillade of automatic fire from its back as it rocked to a stop across the road. Cline and Dooley sent several disciplined short bursts in return, and the truck crashed through a clumsy, tyre-stripping, five-point turn before roaring off the way it had come, its passengers tumbled into a heap.

"We got them, Major."

"Fuck off, Bomber, they pissed off because they were shit scared." Dooley fitted a fresh belt to the M60, letting its loose end hang free down to his knees.

The heat drove Libby back, forcing him to abandon his attempt to save a case of ammunition. A moment later machine gun rounds began to cook-off inside the Black Hawk, and they all had to duck as some came out through the bubbling alloy skin of the fuselage.

Revell tossed a sack of rifle grenades to the armourer. "We've got all we can carry. Everyone take a maximum load. If things are as screwed up as they look, then we won't be able to count on much in the way of re-supply."

They were fifty yards from it when the helicopter's fuel tanks ruptured and exploded. Libby saw the mini-gun, the section of floor to which it was bolted, and a shower of ammo boxes sail across the street to crash into and through the wall of a warehouse.

A gunship spun into the road ahead of them, disintegrating and filling it with fire that instantly spread to the timber yards on either side. Sergeant Hyde struck off down a side alley, and the others followed. They had to step over a man-sized depression in the asphalt that was filled with a stinking red pulp. Tangled white silk draped a stack of oil drums close by, linked to the remains by twisted rigging lines.

The alley ended at a wire mesh fence. Through it, made indistinct by the clouds of drifting smoke, Libby saw their objective. It looked different from the aerial photographs. The bare cement walls had been toned down by the application of a wash of camouflage paint, but the control-towerlike glass top was unmistakable. Steel shutters had been added, but had been left folded back. From where they stood, at ground level, it was impossible to be sure, but at least ten, and possibly twenty or more long lines of assorted railway wagons separated them from the signal cabin.

"Sure is a pity the major can't do a Moses, and get these freight cars to part for us."

"Just get us through the fence." Cline slapped his cutters into Ripper's hand.

"Shit, how come you're always giving me the work?"

"Every time you open your mouth, you draw attention to yourself." Clarence volunteered the answer as he worked at the other side of the opening, cutting through the woven intersection of the wire to work at twice the young infantryman's speed. He had to brush aside Boris's attempts to help. The Russian was nervous and, hampered by the whipping aerial of his manpack radio, only managed to get in the way. His nervousness showed in the taut lines in his slab face and his fumbling eagerness to get the squad moving once more.

From the far side of the yard came the sounds of small-arms fire, and further away, the fast punching crack of multiple cannons.

"In we go." Revell went first, and stood guard as the others and their loads were fed through. His first glance had told him there was no choice of route. To go around the long lines of wagons would have taken too long. They would have to thread through them, squeezing between each row into what was a potential killing ground if there were any more militia in the area. And by now there was a strong chance there would be.

Andrea sent a long burst at a brown-uniformed figure that sprinted from a small shed. The last few bullets caught him, and the man went down, kicked once then lay still. "A Russian. They said nothing about Russians."

"Probably just railway troops, bound to be a few. Burke, get me his jacket."

"I'll get it." Before Burke could act Dooley had set down his machine gun, and was running towards the body, spare belts flapping about him.

A second figure appeared at the door of the shed, then ducked back as Libby fired from the hip, a brief burst that went nowhere near its target, but drove the Russian back out of sight before he could take aim with a pistol.

Not bothering even to attempt to remove the jacket, Dooley grabbed the corpse by the wrist and began to tow it back, sweeping a broad stroke on the damp ground that was marred by the indents made by the trailing boot heels.

The shed blew apart, first being lifted from its foundations, and then collapsing inwards like a card house, as Andrea's 40mm rifle grenade went in through a window.

Mud and blood had to be wiped from the corpse's sleeve patch before Revell could decipher its design.

"Well, is he railway troops?" Burke pushed forward, trying to see past Sergeant Hyde.

"No, artillery." Turning the body over with his boot, Hyde reached into an unbuttoned pocket and took out the Russian's pay book. He handed it to Boris. "Does this tell us any more?"

Flicking over the well-thumbed pages, Boris stopped at those detailing the soldier's specialist training. "He is with an air defence regiment."

"No bloody wonder they're hacking our choppers out of the sodding sky. This shit must have a load of mates around here. No one said anything about all this bloody flak. A bloody milk run they said. It's fucking Arnhem all over again."

Burke watched as Dooley roughly cut away the badges from the dead man's jacket. "I wondered what had made you so keen. You started souvenir collecting?"

"Yeah, sort of. Fetch a good price do these, from the typewriter warriors back at HQ." He cursed at having to leave the belt buckle, as Hyde shoved the M60 at him, and pushed him after the others.

As Libby moved from the security of one line of wagons to another his mouth was dry and his breath came faster. Beneath the big steel-bodied cars nothing could touch him, but each time his turn came to wriggle into the open, drag his rifle and pack out after him then dash the few feet to the next sanctuary, before repeating the same frantic process in reverse, fear struck him in a way that was almost physical. He watched Clarence when his turn came. The sniper's coolness made him as devoid of expression as the hideously disfigured Sergeant Hyde, but there was nothing in his actions, no extra caution, no hesitation, to betray even a suggestion of fear.

There were fewer choppers going over now, but the sounds of battle around the yard were increasing, with several more heavy weapons coming into action. The crash of grenades was becoming more frequent, and then they heard the first thunder of demolition explosions, and mushrooms of smoke and debris soared high above the yard from the direction of the engine roundhouse.

The concealment offered by the rolling stock ended a good seventy-five yards from the signal cabin. Between it and them gleamed several sets of tracks, woven into a complex junction at the throat of the yard. Stray shots had chipped the reinforced structure, making a couple of star-surrounded holes in the smoked glass windows, but the indicator lights on the modern control board inside could still be seen, blinking on and off.

"We'll put down smoke."

"Hell, Dooley, you hear the major? Ain't enough your big feet are gonna have to trip the little ol' light fantastic over all that ironmongery, he's gonna make you do it with your eyes tight closed, or as good as."

"Shut it, Ripper." Hyde had been scrutinising the wagons of a train standing some fifty yards on the other side of the cabin. "I think we can save some rounds, Major." He pointed out from beneath the bulk cement carrier to a pair of unmarked matt-black tanker wagons.

"It's worth a try, and the wind's in the right direction." Revell nudged Libby, and indicated the cleaner of the two wagons. "Five rounds."

"Like shooting at a barn. Reckon he'll hit it?" This time Ripper didn't need to be told, he saw Revell looking his way, and shut up instantly.

Five sparkling spouts came from the evenly spaced punctures made by the high-velocity bullets. "Looks like aviation gas. Try the next in line, same again."

This time the spurting fluid was darker, splashed less where it landed.

"That's what we want, some nice heavy stuff. OK Andrea, put an incendiary grenade into the side of the first one."

It was almost point-blank range, and she had only to elevate her rifle a fraction for the tube of the grenade thrower slung beneath the barrel to put a phosphorous round into the centre of the target.

The detonation of the leaking kerosene mixture was instantaneous. There was a rippling flash of pale flame, barely visible even against the dark paint of the tanker, and then a massive report as the wagon bucked violently and twisting pillars of fire sent its top-mounted valves and inspection hatches hundreds of feet into the air above the marshalling yard. Almost the entire contents were consumed in that moment, but where the gushing liquid had mixed with the glutinous mass from the next wagon it burned longer.

Thick black smoke began to billow about the signal cabin and drift across the tracks towards the squad, as the heavier fuel started to burn in earnest, showing a curling angry red at the base of the pall.

An arm-waving figure appeared at a doorway in the otherwise blank walled base of the cabin. Chased by a flurry of hastily aimed shots, it dived back inside and the door slammed shut.

Cline was the first to reach the building. He fired a burst from his Colt Commando at the now closed door, forcing the others to dive to the ground to find shelter from the wild ricochets that whined and bounced from the thick metal and its strengthened surround.

"Mad arse." Dooley was astounded to look up and see the bombardier still in one piece. "Shit, you should be more full of holes than a fucking colander."

"All of you. Take cover. Libby, get us in there."

Libby took a wad of plastic explosive from his

pack and worked it in his hands to make it more pliable, before pulling it apart, and moulding each of the chunks against the door's exterior where experience told him the bolts were most likely to be. He used a fuse with the shortest possible delay, and barely had time to join the others behind an angle of the structure before it blew with an eardrum-punishing roar.

Hyde had to barge Cline aside before he could toss the concussion grenade through the opening. Dust and smoke swept back into his face and the major used the second it took him to recover to pass him and go in first.

Half-hidden beneath the flattened door lay the partially dismembered body of an East German railwayman. His blood had made the floor slippery and Revell almost fell as he reached for the splintered handrail and started up the concrete stairs three at a time, with Cline hard on his heels.

A single fluorescent tube still lit the windowless room. As it swung, its flickering light made weird shadows of the rack upon rack of relays, switches and other electronic equipment. Another flight led to the control room. The door at its top was closed.

Shouldering his assault shotgun, Revell fired twice and even as the gouged and shattered door crashed back, was racing up to, and through it.

A single hand frantically waving a soiled handkerchief was the only obvious movement among the huddle of four figures in a corner. There was a woman among them, as white-faced as the men, her eyes staring from behind thick lensed glasses.

"Down." Revell demonstrated his meaning by

jerking the barrel of his 12-gauge towards the floor. The cabin staff understood and dropped as if pole-axed, laying stiff and unmoving. "Set the charges, I want this place ready to blow in ten minutes, and get Boris up here. I want to find out how many of the others have made it down safely." Leaving Cline to guard the prisoners, he took advantage of their elevated position to try to get some idea of what was happening in the rest of the yard.

There were several big fires around the perimeter of the area, but whether they were the results of the efforts by other assault groups, or simply marked the sites where choppers had crashed in, it was impossible to tell. A handful of smaller blazes had started among the long rows of rolling stock, and a large cloud of oily smoke was beginning to rise from the direction of the machine shops. That had been a prime target, it had to be the result of demolition.

"I cannot raise any of the other groups, Major." Before reporting that fact, Boris had taken the precaution of checking that the radio was working perfectly. Forestalling the officer's inevitable question.

"Probably too busy to answer, that's all. Keep trying." A burst of machine gun fire came in through the window above Revell's head, and he hunched up to protect himself from the shards of glass that rained on to his helmet and shoulders. "How's the work going? I want us out of here."

Having used his bayonet to prise off the access panels beneath the room-wide diagrammatic train indicator board, Libby was placing lumps of explosive against the thick, variously coloured, multistranded cable runs threading their way through the floor. Fuse wire linked them to those already set beneath the switch-laden control console. "Almost finished here." Gathering the wires together, he began to lead them towards the stairs. "I've saved some for those racks in the room below. When this lot goes they won't be controlling any more trains from here, not for a long time. Be easier to start fresh than unscramble the fry-up I'm planning."

All the time he'd been working, Libby had been conscious of the fact that the East German cabin staff were watching his every move. One of them, he couldn't tell which, but thought it was the oldest of the men, had urinated. A yellow puddle spread sluggishly over the boot-imprinted floor.

"These dumb buggers are shit scared." Cline stood over the prisoners, his rifle aimed at each in turn.

"So would I be if I were them." Stripping the insulation from the ends of the wires, Libby started splicing them together. "Fifteen minutes ago the poor sods were non-combatants in cosy reserved jobs, now they're front line cannon fodder and probably think we intend to leave them here when we blow this lot." A thought struck him, and he glanced at Revell. "Will we?"

"No, the orders say minimum civilian casualties. We'll herd them clear before we go."

Burke clumped up the stairs, not coming all the way into the room, but stopping about halfway, so that his face was on a level with the floor of the control room. He ducked as a spent cannon shell crashed through the last intact pane, pounded a dent into the top of the indicator board and bounced to the floor, to spin to a stop inches from his nose. "This place is a ruddy death trap. How soon before we get out? I'd rather take me chances in the open."

A heavy explosion rocked the cabin, sending a hail of metallic debris clanging off the outside walls, and tumbling Burke back down the stairs. As the thunder of the shock wave passed, his aggrieved voice floated up to the control room, his words bracketed by obscenities.

"And then again, maybe not."

FOUR

"Didn't get far, did they?" As Ripper watched from behind the cover of the pile of prefabricated gantry sections, one of the East German signal cabin staff staggered to his feet, trying ineffectually to stem the gush of blood from the stump of his left arm. He tottered a few steps away from the fragment-slashed and mutilated bodies of his companions, violently spewed an arc of bright red blood and collapsed.

"Perhaps they are better off like that." Andrea had seen the grenade burst among the group. Lobbed by an unseen hand from behind a hopper wagon, it had exploded at shoulder height, tearing them apart. An eyeless head decorated the top of a junction box and sightlessly contemplated her disembowelled torso through broken spectacles. "Better that than be rounded up by the KGB after this is over. Their involvement would have been assumed automatically. Their deaths would have been as bloody but not as swift."

The rapid series of explosions had cracked the

41

walls of the signal cabin, and from the long fissures and its roofless top came flames of every colour as cables and electrical components burned, the copper and plastics running molten down the concrete.

"Don't bother watching for the second wave." Revell knuckled his eyes in an attempt to counteract the itching caused by the sulphurous smoke. "They must have seen the beating we took, sustained heavy losses themselves and turned back. We're on our own, and the word is that includes finding our own transport home."

"Has Boris been able to make contact with any of the other groups?" The reams of figures that had been thrown at them during the briefings came back to Hyde. "We can't be the only assault group on the ground. There were thirty choppers in the first wave, that's better than three-hundred and sixty men."

"Maybe there's a few others milling about down here, but listening to Sky Control, and reading between the lines, I'd say we made one of the better landings."

"Is there to be no pick-up? We are stranded here?" Revell could read the fear in Boris's face. The Russian had good cause to be terrified. For the others in the squad, if they were taken prisoner, it would be a quick bullet in the back of the neck, or if they were lucky, if that was luck, six or seven months of forced labour in a Soviet mine or quarry before they died of malnutrition and mistreatment. For the Russian deserter it would be worse: given the skilful barbarity of the Communists, immeasurably worse.

"Right first time." Having stripped the protective seals from the tube ends of an M72 rocket launcher,

Dooley extended it and flipped up the sights. "You saw the shit we came through, and then they were just warming up. They'll be thoroughly awake now. Those flak and missile battery crews would just love another crack at our whirlybirds."

"I wasn't expecting this to be a milk run, but Christ . . ." Replying to a short burst of submachine gun fire from the vicinity of a burning refrigerated wagon, Burke was gratified to see a brown-clad body topple forward and start to steam in the heat of the conflagration close by. ". . . someone, somewhere has screwed us good and proper. We flew over a couple of complete air defence regiments at least. How come they hadn't been spotted and the warning passed on to us? I tell you, it's like fucking Arnhem all over again."

"Forget the history lesson, though maybe for you it ain't history, you're old enough to have been there: what I want to know is where do we go from here, and how soon?" Putting down the launcher, Dooley used the M60 to send a spray of bullets towards the roof of a distant warehouse. "Shit, missed the bastard."

Taking a little longer to aim, and firing only a single shot from his Enfield Enforcer sniper rifle against Dooley's twenty, Clarence brought down the Russian.

The man held on to his binoculars as he fell the sixty feet, legs kicking wildly, to land out of sight. Another who had been climbing along the ridge to join him, panicked, lost his grip, and disappeared over the far side.

Their Russian radio-man was still waiting for an authoritative answer. Revell could feel Boris's eyes on him, could feel their intensity like a physical thing. "They would just be throwing the crews' lives away."

"What of our lives, what of ours?" Boris thumped himself in the chest, striking hard with the inside of his closed fist. "They sent us first, to test the danger, and now they leave us . . . don't they know what that means?"

"Take it easy." Revell had to hold the frightened man down when he would have leapt to his feet. "OK, so we're not going home by the quickest route, but I still intend us to get there."

"Hey, you kidding us, Major?" Ripper ignored Cline's attempt to stop him from butting in. "This is Indian territory, and we're plumb in the middle of it. Apart from the lil' ol' fact that an army of Reds must be surrounding us by now, and starting to close in, we're a hell of a long way from the Zone, let alone our own lines. We've the best part of a hundred and fifty miles of badlands to cross. By the time we've made it I'll have worn my boots down to the stumps of my ankles. That's if we ever do."

"That layer of dirt on the bottom of your feet ought to be good for at least twice that distance." Bombardier Cline couldn't resist the opportunity offered.

A bullet whined past Revell, cutting the netting on his helmet. He ducked lower. "First thing is to get away from here while there's still a chance of finding gaps to slip through. After that, we'll have to keep moving, think on our feet. It won't take the Commies long to figure out a few of us have got away, and then they'll start a hue and cry that'll have every member of the GDR Politzie, every militia man at a bridge or

44

checkpoint and every Red in and out of uniform keeping a watch for us."

"Be better if we scouted for the openings, rather than all charging about, making ourselves conspicuous." Hyde attempted to inject at least a degree of planning.

"OK, take Burke with you. He's good at wriggling out of work, let's see if we can apply his talents elsewhere."

As the NCO and driver departed, Libby detected a movement under a railway wagon a hundred yards off. The third burst he put into the Russian machine gun team wasn't needed. He felt a hand on his arm.

"Take it easy." Revell withdrew his hand. "There'll be lots more targets yet, save some for them."

Deep inside him Libby felt his emotions whirling in confusion. The ordinary ones of battle were there, the ones he always experienced in combat; fear and excitement among them, but there was another, a new one that kept rising to the fore, swamping all else.

It was a strange burning hatred that was making him kill and want to kill in a way he never had before. Gone was the control, the calm reason that had brought him safely through two years of fighting in the Zone. Replacing it was a growing anger and, mixed in with it, an intense loathing that was aimed not at the enemy, but at himself.

He'd tried, oh God how he'd tried, but he couldn't wipe from his memory that last night of his leave. At most he'd only had a couple of beers, well maybe three, but he hadn't been drunk. No, on that night he had been as cold, as calculating as ever he had been in the heat of battle. All of the old skills had been employed to pick-up the woman, and from the moment he'd begun the familiar process of talking and joking and flirting he'd known what it was he was planning to do.

The marshalling yard wasn't around him any more, he was back in the car, crushing her body with the urgency of his need to come. Every detail was there. It was as far as he could go in satisfying the urges that had grown inside him since Helga had been swept from his reach by the war.

In focusing on her he'd come to detest, to hate other women, because of the temptation they presented. The girlie magazines had fed that hate, and in the car as much as anything else he'd wanted to defile the woman, pumping the product of his massive orgasm on to her clothes to stain and soil them, and doing it there as if to tell her she wasn't worth doing it inside.

There were times, he hardly dared admit it to himself, when the thought had been in his mind, though he'd always suppressed it, that it would have been such a relief to end it all. Forget the search, forget the war and all its horrors and discomforts. He had the means, a choice of methods was all around him. A grenade, or that souvenir Hungarian pistol, either would have done the job . . . but he couldn't do it.

It wasn't that he was afraid of death, provided it came quickly and cleanly; he'd seen many others willingly accept, almost embrace it, and he could understand why. There was a limit to what the human spirit could take, and the pressures he'd been under, both external and of his own making, had been gargantuan, more than anyone should ever have had to bear.

But he hadn't done it, he'd kept going. And he would continue to do so as long as there was a chance, however slight, that Helga still lived. The day, the second, he had irrefutable proof that she was no longer alive he would pull the pin or the trigger, and for a moment experience happiness again before it was all over and he went to join her.

The jump back to reality was abrupt, as a fragment of grenade casing crashed against his helmet. He joined the others in firing on an attempt by a platoon of mixed Russian artillerymen and East German militia to rush them. The last of them to go down were close enough for him to see their faces, and he watched their changes of expression as he went for belly shots.

"Tight as a noose, Major." Hyde dabbed at his cheek. A bullet had slit open the flesh to a depth of a quarter of an inch, but only speckles of blood showed. The exposed tissue had the same pink rubbery appearance as the graft-patched surface of his face. "We did spot another group of our blokes, passed the every-man-for-himself message and invited them to join us, but they weren't interested. They had the same idea as us, to get out and get out fast, figuring a small group stands the best chance.

47

They should have come with us though, the Commies put down a mortar stonk on their position just after we left."

"Have you told him my idea about the transport?"

"Shut it, Burke, I'm making the report."

Burke shut it.

"What transport?"

Sergeant Hyde hesitated. "Well, it's a bit of a long shot. We found an old shunting loco'. It's had a couple of lumps knocked off it, but it's ticking over and seems to be OK."

"You got to be joking." Dooley heaped scorn on the idea. "They ain't like tanks you know. You have to go where the tracks take you. Good chance that'd be straight on to the muzzles of Russian cannon."

"Eh, Major." Ripper had been listening with growing interest. "I got this uncle, he's a switcher with AmTrac, and I used to tag along sometimes. I reckon I know how it's done, if that baby don't go the right way I'll just spike a few blades and make sure it do."

"It's all we've got, let's give it a try." A nagging doubt had occurred to Revell. "Can you drive a locomotive, Burke?"

"Don't know, never tried." He thought he'd better inject a more optimistic note. "But I've never found a vehicle I can't manage somehow. If it works, I'll shift it."

"This war is crazy, fucking crazy." Dooley sent an antitank rocket at a Russian scout car nosing out from behind the shell of the signal cabin. It stopped and began to burn. "We spend half the morning blowing apart the GDR railway system, and now we've got to pray a good chunk of the fucking thing is still working. I tell you, fucking crazy."

"No, leave the wagons coupled. The average Ruskie infantryman is as dumb as they come, but if all he sees is a loco', that's what he'll aim at. If he has a whole train trundling past he may waste shots all along its length." Hyde pushed Cline up into the already crowded cab when the bombardier tried to be the last to board.

Burke flexed his fingers over the controls, like a concert pianist warming up for a recital. "This must be the brake." A loud hiss of escaping air confirmed his guess. "Let's see if I'm as brilliant with the rest. This'll be the first time this crate has been out on the main line, quite an adventure for it. Reminds me of a story I read as a kid, about this . . ."

"We're not on the main line yet, and I don't want to hear about Ivor the Engine, just drive."

If Burke hadn't been enjoying himself he would have taken exception to the sergeant's remarks, but he ignored them, and increased the engine revs as he released the brake. "Here we go . . ."

"Backwards . . ."

The loco' stopped dead, and from behind it, audible above the crackle of small-arms fire and the crash of grenades, came the sequential clanging of the wagon buffers making repeated contact.

"I know, I was just testing . . . trying it out."

"You're trying me." From the cab window Revell blasted three puzzled Russian infantrymen who were openly but cautiously approaching the train. Caught

49

by the merging storm of pellets they were mown down. "Now let's get going."

There was a succession of less violent jerks as the locomotive took up the weight of the loaded hopper wagons in turn, and then they were rolling.

The throat of the yard was dead-ahead, and Burke kept the speed to a steady walking pace as they approached a damaged section of track.

"Keep going, keep going. We've got nothing to lose now."

Not needing the officer's urging, Burke increased the revs a fraction more, and then the wheels were squealing and clattering as the whole machine swung wildly from side to side. Then they were over, and could hear the wagons making the same passage.

The last of the seven-car rake failed to negotiate the section, and slewed sideways, ripping up whole sections of track as it was dragged along, spilling its black load. For a moment it was caught, held back by the jumble of rails and sleepers, and Burke, sensing the sudden resistance, moved the regulator another notch and the screw-coupling broke.

"Hold it." Scrutinising the track ahead, Ripper had seen a set of points against them. "I better do something about that, or we're gonna find ourselves motoring back the way we just came." He opened the cab door. "You all reckon you can provide a mite of covering fire?"

It was needed. Dooley and Andrea jumped out with him, to provide close support, while from the elevated position of the cab the others opened a furious barrage of fire on any other opposition.

A dozen East German militia, unenthusiastic and

unstiffened by Russian troops, broke and ran even as they launched a half-hearted attack, leaving six of their number on the ground.

An anti-tank rocket hit a coal wagon, sending a geyser of dust and dark smoke into the air as the shaped charge easily pierced the metal side and had its white hot fury dissipated among the load beyond. Burning coal tumbled from the roughly circular hole. A second rocket followed and sailed over the roof of the locomotive to self-destruct over a distant row of unmarked wagons. The consequences were near instanteous, and dramatic, as a chain of massive explosions blasted the wagons apart when their ammunition cargoes erupted in spectacular fashion.

Ripper was using a length of damaged track as a lever, but it wasn't until Dooley threw his weight against it that the resistance of the locking device was overcome, and the route opened up once more.

"All aboard." It was a strong temptation to sound the klaxon, but Burke forced himself to suppress it. The urge returned with renewed force as they approached the main line.

Set after set of trailing points were burst open by the locomotive's progress across the junction, and their driver had to move the regulator two more notches to overcome their retarding effect. Sluggishly, the motors responded as they pushed the speed towards the maximum for which they were geared.

A file of Russian combat engineers were crossing the tracks and weren't aware of the train's approach until it was almost on them. Some scattered, tripping and sprawling on the multiple obstacles; others froze and could only stare uncomprehendingly: two died. In their panic they ran into each other and that moment of confusion cost them their lives.

Burke saw the horror in the men's faces as the loco's slab front caught them and they were swept beneath the wheels. Through the daubs and streaks of blood on the windscreen he saw a greater danger ahead of them. The tracks were carrying them straight towards it.

Five hundred yards further on, a lone, old, rust-streaked T55 tank crushed flat a section of the corrugated iron fencing flanking the track, thumped down the three-foot step on to the permanent way and parked broadside on, straddling the steel ribbons running parallel to those taking the train away from the encircled yard.

An officer stood on the tank's engine deck, and he had to move back half a pace to avoid the overhanging stowage bin welded to the turret's rear as it traversed to bring its cannon to bear.

Smoke hid the T55 for a second, and a big ball of orange tracer flashed past the cab to skin the length of the train. Libby could see the Russian officer's urgent gestures, could imagine the tirade of threats he'd be screaming at the vehicle's commander and gunner.

Grabbing their last rocket launcher from the floor, Libby pushed it out through the sliding side window and, against the buffeting of the air and the loco's jolting motion, tried to take aim. It was near impossible, but with the range down to two hundred yards and the tank about to fire again, he had nothing to lose. He sent the rocket on its way.

The flame-tailed missile roared towards its target,

and missed, the small but powerful warhead going on to demolish another panel of the trackside fencing. But the mere sight of it was sufficient for the tank driver. He sent his charge surging forward to get out of the line of fire, and in his panic stalled in the path of the train.

A hand, the major's, clamped down hard on Burke's arm to prevent him reaching for the brake, but their driver hadn't intended to: instead, at the instant he realized collision was inevitable, he rammed the speed selector as far as it would go.

"Hang on." Revell just had time to raise his arm before his face when a shower of broken glass swept into the cab from the shattered windscreen, and he was thrown forward, hard into the controls.

Expecting the restarted tank to get clear in time, the officer remained on the engine deck, and paid dearly for the miscalculation. The loco's buffer caught the rear of the T55 and spun it around. Smashed face-first into the back of the turret, the officer rolled off the hull and was smeared from existence as the armoured vehicle ground over him.

There were more impacts as the third and fourth wagons in the rake also clipped the tank. The last jolt tipped the T55 on its side, so that the tip of its cannon barrel made contact with the overhead catenary system. Fire crackled over the armoured vehicle, the surge of high voltage spot welding its steel hull to the tracks.

A single figure that half-crawled, half-tumbled from the loader's hatch in the turret had the flesh of his face and hands burnt blue, while his leather suit and rib-padded helmet smouldered and charred away in dark flakes.

"We're OK, keep up the speed." Loud grinding noises were coming from beneath their feet, and Revell could see great fans of sparks flying past the windows as the crushed metalwork was worn down against the wheels.

"Shit, we made it. We're on our fucking way home." Dooley tried to dance a little jig with Andrea, but she pushed him off, and he staggered back into Sergeant Hyde.

"Quit it, you fat oaf. Before you start celebrating, take a look."

Turning his face into the blast of cold air coming in through the open front, Dooley saw that they had turned off the main line and were now on what looked like a long-neglected spur heading towards an industrial area. "How the fucking hell did this happen? Where the bloody hell are we going?"

"How the sodding hell should I know, I'm only the driver." As the curve of the branch line became sharper Burke had to ease back the speed to keep the loudly protesting wheels on the track.

"Don't start laying the blame on me." Ripper became conscious of several pairs of eyes on him. "Hell, the lick we were going it were making my eyes go funny trying to watch the track. I tell you what though, I reckon I got a kinda idea where we're going right now."

"Think you might let me know before we run out of track?" Burke had the brakes on hard now, and their fierce application was filling the cab with a banshee scream of metal on metal.

Ripper pointed along the tracks to where they

passed out of sight behind the bases of a row of tall cooling towers. "Looks to me like this spur is taking us back to the place where all that flak was parked. Ain't enough they screwed us up on the way in. Seems that we're about to give them a chance to have another try."

FIVE

"Every fucking time I start to enjoy meself . . ." Applying the brake savagely, Burke brought the train to a halt at the crest of a gentle downgrade.

"All change." The drop from the cab was greater than he'd estimated, and Dooley made a heavy landing on the oil-stained ballast, almost falling.

"You weren't much fucking use were you?" Glaring hard, Burke crammed all of the sarcasm he could into the accusation.

Ripper paused as he turned in the doorway and sought for the top step with his foot. "Heck, now you can't blame me. I seen tidier crows' nests than that tangle of tracks back there a ways. I only said I knew how to spike a point, I didn't offer no guarantees about keeping us heading in the right direction for ever."

"What's the matter?" Squeezing past the driver, Hyde waited his turn to disembark. "Is he complaining about having his new toy taken from him?"

"Sure is. I wonder he don't throw a tantrum and bust it, stop anyone else having fun."

Until Ripper spoke, Burke had been about to grudgingly accept the situation, but now he got an idea, and stubborn: "Major, I take it we don't have a use for this old Commie rattletrap any more."

"Glad you've got the message at last. Now get your carcass out here. We've territory to cover, fast."

Alone in the cab, Burke reached for the brake handle. The motor was still turning over, raggedly, with occasional surges. He'd have liked to have sent it off under full power, but he hadn't the time to rig the controls in a manner that would overcome the built-in fail-safe devices, and so this would have to do. Releasing the brakes, he climbed out to join the others.

"What you been doing in there, saying goodbye to it?" Ripper's boisterous laugh caused his helmet to slump down over his eyes, to leave his broad grin showing.

"Sort of, if you must know." Several seconds elapsed before Burke could be really certain that the wheels were turning, but once he could detect movement, it rapidly grew more obvious.

Trundling with increasing momentum, the locomotive rolled noisily past. Burke felt the warmth of the smoky exhaust, pungent with the stench of unconsumed fuel, and then as the rake of wagons passed, the fierce heat from the burning coal-load of the fourth in line. Red-hot slag tumbled from a circular hole in the side of the wagon, and there were screeches and masses of sparks from a bogie wheel that had jammed. Furnace heat from above sent the white metal of its bearing in dribbles of molten silver globules to splash brightly on the track bed.

The train never made it as far as the cooling towers. Barely a quarter of its journey completed, it rolled violently as it hit a junction. Ballast flew up, and the train left the track. Flying granite chippings were replaced by a spray of mud as the locomotive ploughed to a gentle halt in soft ground flanking the line, its wagons still upright, and coupled, the last of the zig-zag formation clear of the tracks.

Burke tried to grab a launcher from Cline.

"Get your hands off. You want to finish the job then stay behind and tear it apart with your teeth. I'm saving this for the Ruskies."

"Admit it, Burke." Giving their driver a shove that sent him several paces forward, after the others, Sergeant Hyde took a last glance at the wreck, now fast disappearing behind smoke and steam wreathing from the partially spilled load of burning coal. "Today just isn't your day."

"When is it ever. When is it fucking ever."

They hadn't expected to run into Russians so soon, not within a few hundred yards of the tracks, while they were still among the ruins of the abandoned industrial area.

From the glassless window of the dilapidated, almost roofless workshop, Libby could see the back of the big six-wheeled Gaz truck, parked among the piles of scrap metal close to the wall of the old foundry. The building stood on its own, precisely in the centre of the weed-infested, rubble-strewn wilderness they had to cross to get away from the area.

"They been there quite a time, motor's near cold." Ripper returned the pocket infra-red 'scope to Hyde. "Wonder what they're doing out here?"

"It's not what they're doing, but how many of them are there, that's what we need to know." Revell had been making his own examination of the building, but apart from the Russian army vehicle, there was no other evidence that the place was even occupied.

"I can tell you." Among the heaps of rusting castings, Andrea had spotted three tyreless pedal-cycles and a pram-wheeled handcart.

"And so can I." The instant he had seen the truck, tucked from sight in that isolated place, Boris had known why it was there. "It is a black market operation. Once I was involved in such a thing myself. There will be three or four men involved at most. Less would be to invite violence and robbery, a double-cross: more would mean too great a dilution of the profits."

"They make much money at it?" At the mention of money, Dooley's interest had been aroused. He hung on the Russian's words.

"Sometimes, if it is being done on any scale, but usually such things are a once-only transaction, a supply clerk or sergeant taking advantage of yet another administrative error. Only rarely do they get to do it twice. There are many who do well out of spying on their comrades, and word soon gets around. If an officer is involved then he may be able to smother an investigation, but whether he succeeds or not, it will be he who takes the profit, and the men who take the risk."

There was a tight malice-filled smile on Andrea's face. "And it can be a very great risk, if the Russians are not careful. When they are too few in number, or too drunk, or too trusting, my people drive a hard bargain." From its sheath she took her wide-bladed saw backed knife, and sliced a long sliver of iron hard wood from a bench top.

"You want me to scout it, Major?"

"No." Revell took no time to consider the sergeant's question. "No, there isn't the time for refinements. We'll have to hope they're keeping their heads down because of the raid. We'll go in at the run, well spread out just in case they have got a sentry. Some of us will get through. If we reach the building without being seen we'll regroup to cover as many of the doors and windows as we can. There'll be civvies in there so I want a clean job, use knives where you can. Let's go."

There was a hundred yards to cover. A hundred yards of muddy, rotted ground that was littered with foot-catching rubbish invisible among the sprouting weeds and grass. Twice Libby almost fell; the second occasion actually going down on one knee before he recovered his balance. It put him a little behind most of the others, with only Boris lagging further back. There was taut, colour-draining terror on the Russian's face. Terrified of being in the front line, with the chance of sustaining a disabling wound that would mean his being left behind, he was equally frightened of losing contact, of being left on his own behind enemy lines and so he ran at a constantly varying pace, first lagging, then catching up as, in turn, the whirling conflicts of the opposing decisions surged to the fore.

On the far right of the line, Libby saw Hyde run close to Clarence, and then watched the sniper veer further to the flank and drop into cover, already fixing the silencer to his Enforcer as he did so.

Their pace slowed as they neared the objective, first to a jog, and then to a series of low-crouched lopes.

Cline was first to reach the truck, checked its cab and then moved to its rear. With the tip of his rifle barrel he parted the canvas flaps closing the tilt, and jumped back as a dozen large scrubby-leaved cabbages rolled out and fell loudly into the mud.

Seeing the building's side door start to open, Libby leapt forward, but Andrea was nearer, and faster.

Expecting nothing more than East German sneak thieves, the Russian private held his Kalashnikov threateningly, but did not have his finger on the trigger. The surgically sharp blade swept upwards and the soldier's expression was transformed from menace to shocked intense agony.

Already buried to the hilt beneath his chin, Andrea gave the knife a wrenching half-turn and the flow of blood from the soldier's mouth and nose became a torrent that carried with it his severed tongue and shreds of brain matter.

As body and rifle tumbled noisily to the ground

there was a shout inside the building. Hurdling the girl, pulled down by the Russian's death throes and still trying to extract her knife, Libby plunged into the dark chill of the foundry.

Great shapes loomed over him; lumps of soot from the furnace walls showered down as he collided with cobweb-decorated chains hanging from a gantry, unintentionally sending them clanking and jangling against the chipped and heat-coloured brick. The place was filled with the deafening echoes of the multiple collisions; dust, soot and rust fell as a dark rain from the beams high overhead.

As he grabbed at them, and succeeded in reducing the sound to a gentle rhythmic clinking, he heard the shout again. It wasn't a call of alarm, and the words were heavily slurred. Whoever was doing the shouting was too lazy, or more likely too drunk, to come and find out for himself what was going on.

Hearing the others moving into the building behind him, Libby cautiously edged forward into the cavernous interior. Ahead he could see a group of figures squatted about a stack of food on the floor: stepping into the open to challenge them, he was instantly blinded as a far door was thrown open and a brilliant shaft of light streamed into his eyes.

Blinking to try and see through the tears that filled his vision, he could only distinguish the blurred wavering outline of the helmeted Russian who sprang to his feet, discarding a scrawny chicken and grabbing for a rifle.

Another of the group was standing, moving across his dimly-seen target, and Libby held his fire as he recognised a female form. The Russian had the rifle, was aiming, and then pitched forward on to his face as Revell buried a bayonet in his back.

The other who died, his neck broken by the crashing impact of the butt of Dooley's M60, had hardly begun to get to his feet, and the half-empty bottle of vodka he clutched was smashed as he fell.

Herded into a corner by Cline, the East German black-marketeers were a strange assortment of types, and their reactions to their suddenly changed situation were as diverse.

Dooley searched them. The shabbily-dressed old man proved to be only half the width the bulk of his heavy overcoat suggested, once he had been relieved of the twenty or more pounds of cooked sausage he had crammed into various pockets. From the woman, Dooley received a stinging slap across the face when he twice went over her matronly bust. In contrast to the senior citizen her mood was one of annoyance, with no trace of fear.

It was the last of the trio Libby found most interesting. He was young, still in his teens, and well dressed in a flashy way. A smell of cologne wafted from him and his sun-tanned fingers showed tell-tale white bands, where rings he'd thought it prudent to leave behind had left their mark.

Like the woman, he didn't appear scared, but there was something in his manner, a suggestion of nervousness. For a second time Libby noticed the glance he directed towards a distant door.

The others were busy, and leaving Ripper to guard the trio, Libby crossed quietly to the door. Easing it open, ahead of him he saw a long passageway, with several rooms leading off to either side. The first had glass walls, and he could make out drawing-boards and rows of dusty shelves. With the others came more risk, and he listened carefully at each before looking inside.

Reaching the last door he paused, and put his ear to the peeling paint. He knew what it was he could hear, knew, and at one and the same time wanted to burst in and put a stop to it, and stay where he was, listening. In a moment one of the others would follow him. Every cell in his body was pounding as he eased down the door handle and gently pushed it open.

Eyes clenched in straining concentration, the Russian didn't see him. The girl bent over the table did. Between grimaces as the Russian thrust into her backside, she gave a half-smile, that was wiped instantly from her face as she recognised the NATO uniform.

Her scream alerted the Russian, but he only had time to open his eyes before Libby was on him. A fist swung savagely hard broke his nose and spattered blood on to the girl's rump even as his fast-shrinking erection was withdrawn. A second even harder blow burst his right eyeball from his head.

One hand trying to haul up the hampering pants about his knees, the other attempting to palm the squashed mass back into its socket, the Russian sergeant reeled, tripped and fell against the side of a battered filing cabinet, nearly severing his left ear on its razor-sharp edge.

Using his boots and the butt of his rifle, Libby laid into the man as he tried to squirm into a corner and protect himself by drawing up his knees and tucking his shattered face into a foetal position.

Everything that had been inside him for so long poured out of Private Libby. All the frustration and hate was unleashed in a frantic torrent of violent rage that went on and on. He heard bones break, saw spongy brain matter exposed as the skull was crushed, felt firm flesh give like latex foam beneath the crashing fury of his attack.

Wild hysterical screaming from the girl as her half-naked body was splattered with the blood fast smothering the room made a hellish background symphony for the ugly noises of the butchery. Libby only stopped when he had no further strength to inflict damage on the long-dead Russian.

Standing over the sprawled body he could see no unmarked inch of flesh, no recognisable feature on the face, or where the face had been. Turning to the girl Libby realized she had stopped screaming, and now stood whimpering, clutching ineffectually at herself as she involuntarily urinated in sheer terror.

"I won't do it to you, I won't."

She didn't understand his words. Libby wanted to tell her why he had done it, explain. Now she fell to her knees, clenched her wet hands together and with sobs punctuating every word, began to beg.

Oblivious to the foul smells in the room, Libby reached out and gently pulled her to her feet. The action came naturally. He put down his rifle and took out his pistol. He set the safety to "off," chambered a round, and pressed the heavy, warm metal into the girl's hand.

Her body still heaved with sobs as Libby drew her to him, held her close and cradled her head on his shoulder. Feeling her move against him he closed his eyes. She was bringing up her hand, he felt the tip of the barrel brush past his ear, and then the world burst apart with a shattering roar.

SIX

The office was painted with blood. It covered the floor and ceiling, was daubed on every wall and smeared over the few pieces of furniture.

Libby was supporting the limp body of a girl. Half of her head had been blown away and an automatic pistol, held by a crooked finger in the trigger guard, dangled at her side.

Revell crossed the room and took the weapon from her nerveless grasp as Libby let her slide to the floor, where she flopped half on to her side, exposing the gaping hole made by the heavy bullet's exit.

"There isn't the time now, but I'll want an explanation later."

"You can have whatever you bloody want." Absently, Libby brushed tufts of matted hair from his jacket front. The action made no discernible difference to his appearance, smothered as he was in the evidence of the violence.

"We've got visitors." Clarence didn't step into the room, delivering the information from several paces outside the door. "A couple of Russian field cars, packed with Commandants Service troops."

"They must be after this crowd." Indicating the flayed Soviet NCO, Revell rubbed grime from a cracked pane and looked out at the pair of open-topped vehicles. They were still the best part of a quarter mile off, picking their way carefully through the broken masonry and debris on the road. "Everyone into the truck."

As Dooley kicked the last of the vegetables from the back of the Gaz, and set up the M60, he found a moment to glance admiringly at the hefty buttocks of the East German woman as she pedalled furiously away from the foundry, then Burke crunched the truck into gear and it took all of his concentration to hang on.

Boris sat between Revell and the driver, his state of mind betrayed by the sweat beading his face, and his nervous compulsive clutching of the radio pack in his lap, so hard that his knuckles whitened.

"Not too fast. I want them to think we're going to stop." Revell had clipped a fresh magazine to his assault shotgun, and now cradled it with the muzzle only a fraction from the open passenger window.

The cars had stopped, blocking the road, and several of their passengers had dismounted and now stood about waiting for the truck. Every one of them was heavily armed, and each held his automatic weapon ready for instant use.

A dwarfish Russian captain stepped forward and held up his hand, a slung machine pistol bumping against his barrel chest. His expression of thuggish arrogance was wiped from his face, at the same second as his confident stance gave way to a hurried backing movement.

The collision hardly caused any check to the accelerating six-wheeler's speed. As the heavy duty front off-side tyre mounted and caved in the chest of the captain, one of the sturdily built field cars was bulldozed away and the other flipped on to its side to trap the three men still in it.

White fire spread among the Russians who had leapt aside in time, as Revell's incendiary rounds sprayed phosphorous and hideous death. To its effect was added the massed fire from the men in the back, and then as they passed, short precise bursts from Dooley on the machine gun.

Wreathed in acrid smoke, the site of the would-be road-block presented a horrific spectacle, with several of the military police reeling in circles, every inch of their bodies being consumed by the unquenchable flames.

Two or three ill-aimed bursts were sent after the Gaz, but the closest passed safely overhead, and only a single bullet actually scored a hit, grazing past the cab to smash a rear-view mirror.

"Turn coming up, Major. Which way?" Burke crunched down through the gears as he slowed the elderly truck. "Christ this thing is knackered. Can we stop and swop it for something else?"

Having at last managed to unwind the twists of wire securing the broken catch of the roof hatch, Revell stood on the seat and looked out. The whole of the horizon to one side was a curtain of variously coloured smoke, occasionally lightened by an ascending fireball as fuel or ammunition cargo ignited in the marshalling yard.

"Keep the pall on your right, and nurse this clunker as best you can." Dropping back into his seat, Revell didn't bother to resecure the hatch, so that it clattered at every bump in the road. "Getting a replacement might not be all that easy."

"If the smoke is on our right," Boris dabbed at his face with his already perspiration-dampened sleeve, "then we are going north. The Zone, and our own lines are to the west. That is the way we must go."

"No." Using his last reloads, Revell replenished the 12-gauge's half-emptied magazine. "It won't take the Ruskies back there long to figure just what's been going down. Soon as they put two and two together and come up with the conclusion that it's us, and not some panicking black-marketeers who did them the damage, they are going to come after us with a vengeance. They'll be expecting us to head west, so we'll try to motor north for a while, until we're clear of the action, then we'll head for the Zone using minor roads."

"Problem up ahead." There was no civilian traffic moving on the roads, but Burke had been forced to reduce speed several times while he negotiated partial roadblocks unintentionally formed by East German drivers who had hurriedly abandoned their vehicles at the commencement of the raid, and had not yet summoned up the courage to return to their charges. Several large articulated trucks had simply been left where they had happened to brake to a stop, with their long semi-trailers sprawled across two-thirds of the width of the wide road.

"Ease back on the gas. We don't want to get tangled up with them." The line of twenty or more well-spaced trucks had also been seen by Revell, but what he had noticed almost as quickly, and had given him much more cause for concern, was the half dozen motorcyclists escorting it. Not content to hold their station, the riders were flashing back and forth along the slow-moving file, constantly waving and signalling to the crews, apparently urging them to greater speed.

"If those wagons are in the same state as this one, it'll take more than a few shouts to get them to roll any faster. Shit, one of the cocky sods is taking an interest in us. Let's hope he can count, and realises we're not one of his."

The motorcycle roared past, executed a tight skidding turn behind them, and suddenly appeared alongside the driver's window. Its rider gesticulated wildly, and shouted at the top of his voice, but was barely audible above the bellow of the Gaz's holed exhaust.

"He wants us to catch up with the others. He thinks we are with them."

Boris gave the translation out of sheer habit, he was beyond reasoned thought as he watched the two-wheeler dart ahead, and saw the machine pistol slung behind the rider's back. "I feel sick."

"Then do it in your damned helmet. Not over me." From the floor Revell retrieved one of the helmets they had pushed beneath the seat as the escort had drawn up alongside, checked it was the Russian's own, and pushed it at him. "And don't do it on the radio either."

Every few moments the motorcyclist would glance back at them, twice making a beckoning gesture.

"You better do as he says. Just keep as much distance as you can between their tail-end charlie and us, without giving them reason to take an interest in us again."

"What happens if they turn east, or stop for a brew?" Burke was trying to judge the distance just nicely, close enough to the convoy to keep the escort happy, but not so close that they'd be under constant scrutiny.

"If and when, we'll play it by ear." Revell looked out of the side window, and pretended not to hear the sounds of their Russian emptying the contents of his stomach.

"Shit, shit, shit." Near-bending the gear lever in his effort to shift to a lower ratio, Burke eventually had to settle for the jerking snatch of dropping two, as the convoy slowed to a crawl. "They're turning off. Oh bloody Christ, look where we're going."

There was no chance to make a break. The first five trucks had already turned into the camp, and half the escort had dismounted to direct the rest of the vehicles off the road. A heavily armed group of military police stood by a BRDM scout car beside the gates and were taking a bored interest.

Boris was sick again, as their turn came to drive into the huge sprawling vehicle park beside the serried ranks of bleak barrack huts, but had nothing left to bring up, and could produce only ugly retching noises and a little spittle.

The guardhouse beside the entrance was a single-storey concrete structure that doubled as a pillbox. A light flak-gun stood on its roof, surrounded by a low rampart of sandbags. Once past it Burke had no choice but to tag behind the last in line of the convoy. The whole place swarmed with Russians, and a large concrete building, unremarkable save for its extreme ugliness, indicated that the place was a headquarters of some sort.

"Flak-outfit." As they motored past rank after rank of soft-skinned transports, further back, outside a large hanger-like shed, Revell noticed two tracked missile systems receiving attention from fitters. "No, keep going."

Burke didn't need any urging. Instead of parking in line alongside the other trucks, he kept straight on. "Have you seen the fence around this place? There's no way we can crash through in this crate, all we'll do is pull up a few posts, wrap ourselves in barbed wire and make a hell of a lot of enemies."

"We've got those already. Steer for that building at the end of the next block. The one with the green roof, standing a bit on its own."

Bringing the truck to rest beside a huge radio van that looked as if it was either in the process of being built from spare parts, or itself being cannibalized for spares, Burke had a twenty-second fight with the gears to find neutral, and eventually gave up and turned off the engine, keeping his foot on the clutch until the last shuddering over-run had ceased.

"Someone is coming to tell us off for parking in the wrong place."

The clipboard waving junior sergeant was shouting at the top of his voice, and going red with the effort of doing that at the same time as jogging towards them.

Waiting until the man was only a couple of yards from the cab, Revell hurled the contents of Boris's helmet from the window. A little spattered back inside, but most of it went over the clipboard, and the junior sergeant's boots.

For a long moment the insulted individual just stared, then whirled on his heels and ran back the way he had come.

"He's gone to fetch us trouble."

"At least it's bought us time. Get Boris out, I'll collect the others." Time; they needed more than time. Now a miracle would have been useful. Revell recalled his own words to Sergeant Hyde, earlier in the day, about thinking on their feet. Well, look where it had got them, not to safety, but right into the heart of an enemy camp. It was too late now, but maybe Hyde had a point, about the need to find the time for at least a degree of planning. But that wasn't Revell's way, oh no, he just went charging on . . . well the charging was about to end. Any moment now the Russians would wake up to what was happening in their midst, and then the end would be swift and bloody. He would have to make a point of staying close to Andrea, save a bullet or a grenade for her. She would not do it for herself, not while there was still a chance of one Russian presenting himself as a target.

"Looks like we jumped out of the frying pan and locked ourselves in the oven, Major." Hyde was already ushering the others from the back of the Gaz. He indicated Boris, who, in a state of collapse, was

76

having to be supported by Ripper and Burke. "What's the matter with him, has he been hit?"

"Just scared silly."

"Ain't we all." Ripper's helmet was knocked back, to reveal his spotty forehead. "Reckon you've found a cure for my acne, Major. Pretty soon some Ruskie is gonna come along and blow my head off."

"There's a squad of heavies coming." First to spot the approaching Russians, Clarence looked about for a useful place of concealment.

Hyde had already found one, an empty vehicle workshop . . . well, almost empty. When the others squeezed through the narrow opening between the tall sliding door, they also had to step over the corpse of a fitter whose head lay at an unnatural angle to his spreadeagled body.

"What a beauty, what a bloody beauty." Going up to the big BTR-60 armoured personnel carrier that was the only vehicle in the place, Burke ran his hands over the meticulously applied three-colour camouflage finish, then walked round it, touching each of the eight brand new tyres in turn and enthusing about its lavish equipment. He completed his tour of the massive battle-taxi. "Have you ever seen one of these brutes in this condition, ever seen any Ruskie or Warsaw Pact transport in this condition?"

"It'd make short work of the fence." Libby was more practical in his appraisal of the eight-wheeler.

"The search seems to have moved away." Clarence made his report from the door.

"They will be back."

That the girl was right, Revell didn't doubt for a moment. What the Russian character lacked in capacity for initiative was more than compensated for by an ability to apply sheer mindless persistence to any situation. And if the cause of that determination was a vindictive lust for revenge then it became all the stronger. When the Soviet NCO got over his first burst of passion, and stopped darting about at random, he was going to commence a very thorough search of the area.

"Into the carrier." Revell knew they had nothing to lose, were as good as dead if they didn't burst out. They would still have the element of surprise on their side for a few minutes longer, but as the hue and cry spread that would vanish. It had to be now or never.

The others wasted no time in boarding, clambering up the APC's hull and climbing in through the small side doors and roof hatches. Two of them had to assist Boris, who was incapable of doing anything for himself, so great was the state of shock he was in. Hyde held back, to help with the heavy doors.

Starting at the third attempt, the armoured vehicle's engines filled the shed with noise and pungent black exhaust fumes. As they did, the pair threw themselves at the doors and a growing wedge of bright sunlight flooded in, making beams through the smoke.

Burke set the APC rolling as the last man boarded. "You hear these motors? This crate must belong to someone very fussy, or very special. The mechanics must have spent hours on them. They usually run like asthmatic steam engines."

Having boarded by a rear hatch, Revell went forward to the commander's seat beside the driver, and was slowed by having to thread his way past the gunner's seat suspended from the turret above the middle of the single narrow compartment, and already occupied by Libby. By the time he got his first look out through the forward vision port, their driver was already setting an erratic course among the various vehicle parks and workshops.

"I'm bloody lost, this place all looks the same to me. Where's the fucking perimeter?" Having to brake hard and swerve to avoid a petrol tanker that pulled out in front of them, Burke recognised a feature and got his bearings as they turned on to the new heading. But it wasn't the one they wanted, and with serried ranks of close-spaced huts and parked trucks and field cars to either side, there was no way he could turn off.

Having at last in the cramped confines of the turret managed to feed a belt of mixed armour-piercing and incendiary rounds into the 14.5mm heavy machine gun, Libby looked out through the sight aperture, and immediately chambered a round.

Ahead was the gate by which they had involuntarily entered. The scout car had been joined by a pair of T62 tanks, and as the gun crew manning the flak-position on the roof of the guardhouse saw the APC approaching they began frantically traversing their weapon.

SEVEN

Russian troops were pouring from the guardhouse as Libby made ready to open fire on the flak-mount. There was nothing he could do about the tanks, but by Christ he'd take some of that gun crew with him.

"Hold your fire."

The major's order crackled over the headset at the same moment as Hyde shook his ankle to get his attention, and shouted the same thing. When Libby looked again the scene at the gate was transformed.

In front of the guardhouse an officer was hurriedly marshalling a line of troops, while the gun crew had all stood to attention. One of the tanks was backing off to make more room at the gateway.

As the APC neared, the officer called his men to attention and they presented arms and he saluted as the stolen vehicle swept past and out on to the open road.

"This wagon is done up like a mobile whorehouse." Dooley tried one of the leather-upholstered bucket seats that replaced the thinly padded benches normally a feature of those spartan vehicles.

"Hey, now there's a real neat idea. I heard of a floating crap game, but the idea of sex on wheels, I like that." Ripper thumbed through a rack of magazines. Several were western publications. Between the latest copy of *Pravda* and *Red Star* were a *Playboy* and two *Mayfairs*.

"I think this might explain things." Clarence took a bright coloured square of embroidered cloth from a small locker and held it out for the others to see.

"Pretty. What is it?"

Clarence snatched it out of Ripper's reach, to prevent it being covered with filthy fingerprints.

"You ought to do your homework." Dooley leant forward, to try to look in the locker. "That is a general's pennant. It could explain why we got the red carpet treatment, in fact I guess it does. Anything else in there?"

"Help yourself." Clarence moved aside to let the big man rummage excitedly through the contents.

"I can get a fortune for these, and look at this, it's . . ." Suddenly Dooley became secretive. "I ain't sharing." Items he took from the locker were transferred to his pockets with clumsy attempts to conceal them. He kept alternately chucking and peering round suspiciously, as if expecting the others to attempt to pilfer his trophies.

Most of the traffic on the road was military. Burke was careful to keep to the same speed as the vehicles around him and they weren't bothered by the traffic police who constantly patrolled on noisy mud-plastered motorcycles.

Not all the other road users were so lucky. Twice they passed trucks that had been ordered off the road for checks, and saw their drivers being pushed and bullied about while papers were scrutinized.

They were forced to slow as they passed a field where a Chinook helicopter had crashed. The cabin had broken in half on impact, leaving the rear portion little more than a low ash white hump at the centre of a circle of scorched grass. Only the remains of the engine stood above the fused and melted aluminum of the airframe.

From the shattered front portion of the craft a group of laughing East German pioneers were dragging the bodies of the flight deck crew, using meat hooks.

The drivers and passengers of other vehicles on the road were leaning out of their cabs and shouting encouragement, and Hyde had to physically restrain Cline from firing his rifle from one of the side gun ports.

"We can't help them now. You want something to do, then take the radio over from our gibbering Ruskie. He's in no fit state to use it at the moment."

Dooley made a great show of sympathy towards the bombardier, spoiling it by grinning broadly as he did so. His words also lacked sincerity. "Now ain't that a shame, Bomber, and just as we were getting used to your funny little medal-hunting ways."

"What do you mean?" Not made happy by what he saw as relegation to a less than glamorous job, Cline was in no mood to put up with Dooley's sarcasm.

"Oh nothing, nothing much. It's just that this unit

gets through radio-men like you wouldn't believe. Mind, with your self-destructive urges maybe you'll last longer that way. You're hardly likely to charge the Ruskies, threatening to deafen them with a burst of static."

Gradually the traffic flow built up speed once more. As the APC neared the top of a gradient it gave a jolt, and the note from one of the twin rear engines faltered. As they topped the crest it happened again, and this time both units cut in and out erratically.

"Hang on." As Burke called the warning he wrenched the steering wheel hard over and the APC rolled on its suspension as it left the road to turn on to a deeply rutted and potholed farm track.

With the squad all shouting, and trying to secure handholds to prevent themselves being hurled about, their driver put the eight-wheeler through another tight turn.

Bodies and equipment crashed about filling the crew compartment with noise and confused movement and loud cursing and swearing. Only Libby in the turret gunner's seat managed to hold on, and he made several hard contacts with the many angles and projections in the steelwork about him.

With a final pounding bounce the APC stopped.

"Everybody alright?" Burke had to duck a barrage of water bottles, magazines, helmets.

"You mad sod." It took three attempts before Cline managed to regain his sense of balance, his feet and something of his dignity. "What the bloody hell were you trying to do?"

"Don't fucking blame me. The major said to get off the road when we ran out of fuel. Just be grateful we'd made it to the top of the hill. It would have been a bugger sight more hairy if I'd had to do it backwards."

"OK, quiet. Let's see where we are." Revell unfastened the hatch above his seat and stood to look out.

Considering they'd had little choice in its selection, their situation was quite a good one. They were out of sight of the highway, in the centre of a strip of woodland running beside a dirt track, that led to a cluster of neglected barns and machinery sheds grouped about an old stone farmhouse, lower down the steep hillside. He was about to duck back when he heard the squeal of approaching trucks, and the creak and crack of trees going down before a heavy vehicle.

"Diesel. Wouldn't you know it." Dooley tossed the filler cap away, not bothering to replace it on the elderly Blaw-Knox bulldozer.

Utterly confused, and obviously not understanding a single word that was said to him, the machine's equally ancient driver at last got some glimmering of the meaning of Cline's urgent pantomine and climbed down from his rollcage-protected seat to join the two middle-aged surveyors who were already having their hands tied.

Andrea was doing a thorough job of securing their bonds. She felt a tap on her shoulder, it was Revell.

"Go with Sergeant Hyde. I want you to get us some gas. We can hardly trot along to the nearest Commie fuel dump and ask for a few cans, so you'll have to try a spot of highway robbery. It'll have to be done without attracting attention. You've the equipment that should enable you to sucker a couple of truckers."

"Shall I expose my . . . equipment, or do you prefer I simply flaunt it?"

She was taunting him, Revell knew that. "Just get the gas, I don't care what you do."

"I do not believe that, but I will get it for you."

The bitch. The damned bitch. She must by now know how he felt about her and yet, at best, she still treated him with mild amusement. More often she ignored him, though he'd never known her to refuse or be slow to act on any order he gave. There were some he'd like to give her that weren't in any drill manual. Probably, though, she'd end up ordering him. Maybe that would be . . . No. No, his thoughts had strayed that way before and he didn't like the dark depths to which they led. He didn't go in for that sort of thing, hadn't ever . . . wouldn't . . . but if he did . . .

There was a loud excited whoop from the APC. Damn it, what the hell was Dooley up to now? He hurried over, before the big clown made more noise.

"I'm rich, Major. I'm rich. Oh, look at it, look at it."

Dooley was huddled beside a small safe that had been concealed behind a false locker front. From it he had taken, and spread on the map table beside him, several large bundles of bank notes, each a different currency and most from the neutral nations around the Zone; a small collection of stone-jet jewellery, among which a superb diamond cluster ring stood out; two slim carved figures in what looked like near-flawless jade, and a gold bar.

The bullion had been cut in half in order to fit the hiding place, and the residue from that operation had been carefully preserved in a corked test-tube.

"I'm rich I'm rich I'm rich. Oh, I'm rich . . ."

"Shut up you big oaf." Revell was interested in the find, but not for the same reason. His interest lay in the fact that the discovery of the handsome nest-egg tended to confirm the mental image of the vehicle's owner that was forming in his mind.

The pennant already told him the man was a general, but the way the APC was fitted out with luxury touches told him that the Russian officer was also a man of ambition, who wanted the good things in life. His cache of various currencies also betrayed the fact that he was a realist, and not the sort to go down with a sinking ship. Not that the Warsaw Pact forces were losing the war, but this man was prepared for any eventuality.

Having examined the compact but powerful radio equipment on board, Revell also knew that the general had some Western tastes. A radio operator, perhaps one with a less than perfect memory, who did not want to incur the commander's wrath by being slow, had carefully marked certain frequencies on the dial. Revell knew them, they were British and West German civilian radio station frequencies.

"I get to keep it, don't I, Major?"

"Take the notes and jewellery if you want, but leave the bar where it is. Even you can't tote that much extra weight around with you."

Like a child who had just had the cherry stolen off

the top of his cake, Dooley looked very unhappy. He pocketed the other items. "Maybe just one half, Major?"

"Don't get greedy, Dooley. You've enough there to get that pig-rearing farm when you get out, with something left over to treat your *frau*."

Although he brightened a little at the thought, Dooley still cast wistful glances at the safe as the portions of bullion were replaced and the buckled door slammed to wedge it tight closed.

"Truck coming, Major."

In response to Clarence's call through the open hatch, Revell climbed out, in time to see Hyde steering a trailer-towing fuel tanker down the track. Andrea rode on the front fender, holding on to a headlamp bracket. Her jacket was open and her breasts bounced noticeably at each bump.

While a hose from the bowser was being unreeled to the APC, Revell took the sergeant aside.

"Fast work. How did you do it?"

"I didn't, she did."

As he moved to walk away, Revell tackled Hyde on the subject again, trying desperately to be casual, not too insistent, and knowing he was failing.

"What did she do?"

"She took off the combat gear and ran in front of the first truck that was travelling on its own. It just happened to be a bowser."

"And?"

"It stopped." Hyde tired of the game, he'd known what the officer was after all along. "She had on just a pair of white knickers and a tight white T-shirt; she doesn't wear a bra, and what do you think? It stopped, a bloody armoured regiment in full cry would have stopped. She's the most beautiful bloody thing I've ever seen; I nearly went to help her." Hyde couldn't keep the bitterness from his voice. "Next time you want her to do something like that, send her with someone else, not me. I got a face that still upsets nurses in plastic surgery wards. I don't want to see what I can't have."

Hyde turned away, then back. "Oh yes. When the truck stopped she jumped on to the step and cut the driver's throat from ear to ear. He's still in there, that's why she rode on the front."

They had turned off before what looked like a security checkpoint about a mile ahead, and on the quiet side road were now making better speed, and at last heading in the right direction.

Ripper had fastened the general's pennant to the front of the APC, and the few military vehicles they met coming the other way on the narrow road went to extraordinary lengths to get out of the way. In the case of an airforce truck that included a hundred-yard detour through a freshly ploughed field.

Their better progress was having a therapeutic effect on Boris. He still looked ill, appeared to have aged ten years in the last few hours, but had now gathered himself sufficiently to try mumbling apologies for his previous behaviour to anyone who would listen.

". . . you do not know what it is like." Boris kept shifting position so that he could keep looking Clarence in the face, "to live every moment of your life in fear, and then after once making a decision that takes courage, to find yourself hurled into the clutches of the monster that gave rise to the terror in the first place." He caught hold of the sniper's arm, to prevent him from moving away, and then had to nurse the bruised hand that was knocked aside by a sweeping blow with a rifle barrel.

"I am sorry, it is just that I want you to understand. I deserted during an air-raid. It is likely that I am listed as killed. If I now fell into the hands of the KGB, then my family . . . my family . . ."

Clarence watched the Russian as his head dropped into his cupped hands and he broke down and cried. He put his hand forward, to touch the man on the shoulder; for him, so loathing physical contact, it was an unnatural action. His fingers stopped just short of contact, and went no further.

The poor devil. Clarence had been wrapped in his own memories of sorrow and thirst for revenge for so long, he had almost forgotten that the war, the Zone, had brought the same to others. Perhaps for Boris it might even be worse. Clarence had already suffered his loss, there was nothing else that could touch him after that Russian bomber had crashed on his wife and children, nothing that could inflict greater misery, greater torment of mind. But Boris, he knew the Communist system, knew what it could inflict, and knew that he could be the cause of those horrors touching his loved ones. It was a cruel refinement, worthy of the KGB itself.

"Everybody to your position." Revell left his seat and went back to the Russian. "There's some sort of traffic snarl-up ahead. Looks like a queue waiting to cross a bridge. I want you up front. If there's any talking to be done then it's down to you. We're relying on you."

The members of the squad stationed themselves at the firing ports either side of the hull, as they slowed to stop fifty yards short of the tail-end of the waiting line of mixed civilian and military transports.

The single lane pontoon bridge across the Elbe had been blocked by a field car that had jumped the guide rails, and now hung over the swirling muddy water, in imminent danger of falling in.

A recovery crew had backed a truck as close as they could, and were in the process of securing a tow rope, while the endangered vehicle's driver was being pushed and prodded to the far bank under armed guard.

Burke had closed down his front port, and now with Boris looked out at the scene through the thick, scratched and dirt-smeared armoured glass prism filling the vision slit in its metal shutter.

On the far side of the river a group of smartly uniformed Russian soldiers had jumped from a tracked armoured personnel carrier, and as prisoner and guards approached they grabbed the man under escort, forced him to his knees, and a single shot rang out.

"What'd he do? What'd he do?" Burke couldn't believe it. He saw the kneeling figure crumple and watched as the body was shoved with boots and rifle butts into the turbulence close to the bank.

For an instant the corpse bobbed among the white water, then was swept into the main channel, and under.

"He need not have done half so much." Boris felt the fears returning as he recognised the guilty troops. "They are KGB, at once judge, jury and executioners. I doubt whether they bothered to tell him, but that driver would to them have been guilty of sabotage . . ." he paused a moment ". . . no, not even that. It is habit to put labels to what the KGB do, find for them even some glimmer of excuse for their barbarity. Perhaps it was only that he was responsible for delaying them, nothing more than that. Perhaps they are on an urgent mission, but as they are travelling away from the front that is unlikely. The probability is that they are on their way to a brothel, or to pick up some black-market goods . . ."

"And for that they shot the poor shit?"

"They have killed men, and women and children, for far less reason; often for none. If they are prepared to torture prisoners, clear hospitals for their battle casualties by shooting cripples and mental defectives, what chance has some inconsequential East German driver of avoiding their brutality?"

Spurred on by the example they'd witnessed, the recovery section hurried to clear the bridge. Boris watched them risking their lives to complete the task as fast as they could, taking enormous chances above the flood that built to a two-foot wave against the anchored components of the roadway, at times lapping on to them. Steam and smoke billowed from the twin rear wheels of the tow truck as it took up the slack and strained to drag the field car clear.

The moment the obstruction had been hauled from its path the tracked APC drove on to the bridge, forcing members of the recovery section to jump for their lives, several of them landing on the slippery bank, and having to fight and claw their way up it to avoid being carried away by the debris-laden water lapping at their waists.

For what reason, on what whim, Libby couldn't tell, but the carrier didn't drive off the bridge at their end, instead parking itself on the sandbag and tree trunk constructed exit ramp and disgorging its crew once more.

Led by a young and grim-faced lieutenant, the KGB troops began to check the papers of everyone aboard the waiting vehicles, pushing aside the three bridge sentries who had been content until now to sit by the comfort of the small stove beside their guard tent. An unconvincing protest by the senior of the three, and then his offer of help, were brushed aside.

Over his headphones Libby heard the discussion between Revell and Hyde as to their best course of action, and then the sergeant's swearing as their driver reported they were now boxed in by a tank transporter that had pulled up behind them.

The lieutenant flanked by the whole of his section, had started towards the eight-wheeler. "They won't bother with us if they see the general's pennant, will they?"

"The power of the KGB is without limit, and they enjoy it. Look at him." Boris indicated the lieutenant.

Burke could see the young officer's face very clearly, could read in it arrogance and total lack of feeling, but there was something else. The grim look was still there, but something had been added to it. His mouth had drawn up in a tight smile of malicious satisfaction as he approached the captured APC.

"That crud is looking for trouble."

Libby heard Burke's under-the-breath comment, and tightened his grip on the heavy machine gun. "Then let's give him some."

EIGHT

The KGB officer barked a demand for papers, displaying immediate impatience when the APC remained closed-up.

"Sounds as ugly as he looks. What is it about the Commie party that attracts people like that." Unable in the restricted space to level the M60 from the crew weapon ports, Dooley discarded the machine gun in favour of a highly polished AK74 he took from a rack of five behind the driver's seat.

"He's not going away." As he watched, Cline saw the lieutenant summon the rest of his squad. "What's likely to happen next?"

"In a moment he will lose his temper." Boris listened as the shouts were delivered with greater fury. "When that happens he will order his men to open the vehicle and drag us out. What will most likely occur then, you have recently seen." The realisation struck him that he wasn't afraid any more. Even the tirade from beyond the sloped wall of thin armour did not bother him. He had passed through the worst he could ever experience, and it was his turn to feel anger—it was a monstrous towering thing compared with the petty frustration of the KGB man outside.

All these years it must have been growing within him, held back by a wall of fear every Soviet citizen learned to live with from his earliest days. Now the wall was crumbling and the lieutenant was in the path of what was being released.

Forced to the conclusion that his will was not going to triumph, and aware that the incident was making him look a fool in front of his own men, the lieutenant finally snapped, wrenching a grenade from his belt. He took a step towards the APC.

"OK, hit them . . ."

Revell's words were lost in the massed crash and clatter of every weapon aboard the carrier opening fire simultaneously. The lieutenant was hurled backwards by thirty or more impacts that tore chunks of flesh from his body and burst apart the bones of his skull, unimpeded at such short range by the thin steel of his helmet.

Using the turret's heavy armament Libby sent a long burst raking along the side of the file of waiting vehicles ahead of them, and then concentrated his fire on the tracked vehicle blocking their route.

A figure briefly appeared behind a pintle-mounted machine gun on the carrier's roof, then disappeared inside as the stream of tracer-towing rounds smashed into the mount and its shield and ignited the attached box of ready-use belts. Twice Libby swept his fire across the vehicle's hull front, watching rounds bounce from the armour and rip apart every external fitting.

Another Russian appeared from behind the carrier, and was half-hidden by smoke as he sent a shoulder launched anti-tank rocket at the eight-wheeler. He ducked back, chased by a line of bullets, as the rocket's warhead struck short, scattering bloody scraps of cloth and hunks of raw meat as it destroyed a body in the road.

Two of the tracks had begun to burn, and as thick smoke from them and the first few oily black wisps from the KGB vehicle wreathed the road, Burke rammed the APC into gear and sent it surging through the hedge and into the field alongside.

Small-arms fire made a metallic hail on the hull, beat thumping tattoos on the self-sealing tyres. As they pulled clear, a second rocket soared across the ground they had previously occupied and exploded in the cab of the tank transporter.

Once they left the paved surface it was impossible for anyone aboard the APC to fire with any degree of accuracy. Even Libby, with his machine gun firmly mounted, could not stay on a target for more than a second or two as the vehicle's inadequate suspension failed to dampen the effects of the field's undulations.

Burke's evasive driving made no concession to the discomfort of those in the back, as he pushed the speed as high as he could. The APC jumped a wide drainage ditch, landing with a jarring crash, and then still without check to its mad career, crushed a path through a plantation of tree seedlings, the deep-treaded tyres churning broad tracks as they slewed back and forth.

Before a belt of woodland took them from sight of the road a last rocket-propelled anti-tank shell blurred past, missing by only inches, and going on to self-destruct in the unseen distance.

Holding tight to a metal bracket that had twice tried to scoop out his left eye, Boris clutched his rifle in his free hand. The wild ride suited his mood of elation. He could still see the KGB lieutenant's face as he took the first fusillade in the stomach and chest, before the other bullets struck and there was no face left to see. It had felt good, very good. With luck there would be more chances, many many more.

"Ah just love messing about in boats, but shit, paddling across a goddamned river in this old bucket, that just ain't my idea of fun." Ripper stood on the bank surveying the rushing water, as Dooley took his turn with the shovel.

"Who said we're ever going to make it to the water?" Throwing aside a huge sodden clump of soil, wrenched from the cloying ground around the deep-sunken front wheel, Dooley took a hard look at the excavations around the vehicle's other tyres. "Bloody incredible, isn't it? They have the whole of the fucking riverbank to chose from and Burke drives us straight into a shitty swamp." He grabbed a bundle of brushwood from the pile Clarence and Hyde had deposited beside him and stamped it under the wheel, splattering himself in the oozing black mud.

"Heck, this ain't no swamp. You want to see a swamp, I'll take you home with me next time I go."

"What makes you think you're ever going to see home?" Burke dropped another big armful of twigs, then made a hurried retreat back to firmer ground as

Dooley deliberately smacked the flat of his shovel hard on to the glutinous surface. It sprayed the driver from head to foot, and he had to spit out some of the foul-tasting mud.

"You fucking did that on purpose. What you bloody mad at me for? I didn't choose this ruddy place to cross."

"No," Dooley loaded his spade with a generous portion of dripping, rotting vegetation, "no you didn't choose the place, but if you'd bloody been awake you'd have thought to use this crate's tyre pressure regulation system. All you had to do was flick a switch, let a few pounds out and we'd have sailed across. Now piss off before I shove you under one of the wheels."

"Like I was saying . . ."

"I heard what you were saying." Using the edge of the shovel, Dooley rammed more of the brushwood beneath the tyre. "After today I don't ever want to see another swamp. This one may be only fifty yards square but it's plenty big enough to last me for life. I can't think of one good use for a swamp, what you hicks spend all your time in them for, fuck knows."

"They ain't all bad." Taking off his helmet, Ripper set it upside down in a patch of surface water, where it floated, dragging a chinstrap anchor cable. "Hell, some of the best times I've ever had have been in swamps . . ."

"You've got to be kidding." Pausing after dumping more wood, Libby listened.

"Honest I ain't. One time me and my cousin Billy we went and sneaked up on this sort of hideaway Ellen Jane had built right out in the wilds; she was

my aunt, sort of, she'd been married to my Unc' Jeb
before he got himself put away for a long stretch
when he got caught with a load of 'shine, only he
weren't really my uncle . . ."

"Forget the family tree and all the monkeys in it,
get on with the story." Dooley's patience was
wearing thin. He'd slipped for the third time, and
now didn't bother to get up again, sitting sunk to the
waist in the stinking waterlogged ground.

"I was about to. Anyway, Ellen Jane being not
much more than sixteen, she'd gone back home to
live with her Ma and Pa after Jeb went inside. You
know that Pa of hers was a real bible freak, holiest
man I ever saw, even the Reverend Smith used to say
'oh God' when he saw him coming. OK, I'm getting
on with it . . ." Ripper had seen Dooley reaching for
the shovel.

"Me and Billy we reckoned she'd started up a little
still on her own, on account of her having got a taste
for it from Jeb, only when we peered through those
bushes . . . I got a hard on that damned near burst my
zip. She'd finished the best part of a bottle of real
Scotch and were poking the neck of the bottle up
between her legs. Hell, she sure was enjoying herself,
but Billy thought it were a bit dirty to keep taking the
bottle out to have another swig."

"What happened," Dooley was now all attention,
"did you get in on the action?"

"Well after a while she spots us, and acts all
flustered, then she says she'll do things for us if we'll
keep quiet about what we seen. She sure knew what it
were all about. She started sucking me while Billy
tried to take her doggy-style. Only trouble was, he'd

100

not had any practice and he got kinda careless and shoved into the wrong hole. Sure must have surprised her. Next thing I know she's clamped down on my equipment and I'm thinking she's bit it through. I tell you, I still got the marks."

"You'll have some from me in a minute." Revell pushed Ripper aside, so that he staggered back, and sank his helmet. "In case you've forgotten, we're still a long way behind enemy lines, and we've the Zone to cross as well. I want us on the other side of this river before dark. That's one hour. Are we ready to try again yet?"

Dooley looked at the wheels. Pieces of wood, leaves and dried grass kept floating to the surface to form miniature rafts that broke and reformed at every splash and ripple. "Shit, Major, I don't even know if there is a solid bottom under this muck. Maybe we could go on dumping brushwood into it forever without doing a bit of good. One thing is for sure, the APC is still sinking. Another ten minutes and it'll be up to the belly plates, and then no one will ever shift it."

"Then let's try now."

As Burke scrambled up the front of the hull and dropped down through a rooftop hatch into the driver's seat, the rest of the squad positioned themselves around the other three sides of the vehicle.

The engines rumbled into throbbing life, and at the back Dooley and Hyde had to turn away from the choking clouds of unburnt, fuel-saturated exhaust gas.

Its engine revs increasing steadily, the APC nudged forward and the squad threw their efforts behind its attempt to break free.

Away to their left the cloying surface erupted with a roar into a towering geyser of mud, water and vegetation. A second explosion punched a bubbling white cascade from the river, close to the bank.

"Mortars. Keep pushing." Revell put every ounce of strength he had into the attempt to shove their transport clear.

With its broad tyres deliberately deflated so that they flattened further to spread the vehicle's ten-ton weight on the flimsy causeway, it began to inch forward, as two more high explosive bombs, falling almost vertically at the end of their soaring trajectory, bracketed them.

The soft ground that had caused all the trouble in the first place now worked in their favour, as the projectiles' insensitive fuses failed to detonate the explosive filling until the rounds had buried themselves a foot or more, when their deadly fragmentation effect was smothered.

"Keep it rolling."

Now moving unaided, and seemingly likely to maintain its forward momentum, the squad grabbed any projection on the APC's hull to haul themselves aboard, closing the last hatch as a barrage of shells plastered the ground they had left and beat to foam the water about them as Burke drove the APC into the Elbe.

Cutting in the water-jet propulsion the instant the movement of the hull told him they were afloat, Burke still couldn't move quite fast enough to prevent the current from sweeping them downstream.

Through his sights Libby saw each bank in turn as they whirled round, before they came under a degree of control and began to head for the far side.

The mortaring ceased almost immediately as their speed of drift took them out of range, and Libby never even glimpsed the position from which they had come under fire.

"Aren't you going to give them a parting present?" Cline peered up into the turret.

"No one to give it to. I'll save these belts until I can see a target." Despite his answer, Libby almost had unleashed a burst in the direction from which it was almost likely the mortars had been fired, but had recognised the futility of the gesture.

It took seven attempts at five different sites before Burke succeeded in driving the APC from the water, and wouldn't have managed it then if there had not been a small concrete slipway at the bottom of a garden attached to an imposing house.

Gouging deep furrows in the immaculate lawns, Burke drove them around the side of the great gothic structure and on to the raked gravel drive. Past a long line of parked staff cars, they headed for a distant gate, while several lounging East German and Russian airforce drivers watched with gaping mouths, some of them half-saluting as they recognised the bedraggled flag flapping heavily from its miniature mast.

A long Zil limousine, its black paint shining in the rays of the setting sun, had to take a detour through a rose border as the APC refused to give way, showering its gleaming paintwork with stones and dirt.

Taken totally by surprise the guards on the gate hesitated, uncertain whether to present arms or make a challenge, then decided something else had to come first as the eight-wheeler charged through, clipping one of the carved lion-topped pillars, and ripping away its ornamental wrought-iron gate.

"First he drives us into the middle of a Russian camp, then he takes us for a tour of a Staff College or something. You got any other tricks saved up for us?"

Swerving the APC on to the main road, Burke half-turned and winked at Dooley. "That'd be telling."

"Just drive."

"Yes, Major, driving now, Major."

"We are leaving a trail of incidents behind us." Removing his boot, Boris wiped it with a piece of cloth that was instantly stained black.

"That's one way to put it." Hesitating before slipping a half-bar of chocolate back into his pocket, Clarence proffered it to the Russian, who accepted it with a nod of thanks.

"If somewhere they are being plotted, if pins are being stuck in a map, then by now the Communists will know which way we are heading."

"More than likely I would say. I think we got off to a bad start by stealing a general's personal battle-taxi, especially as it turned out he had his nest-egg hidden in it. Didn't he, friend Dooley?"

"How did you . . . I haven't . . . what're you on about?"

"Thanks for the confirmation. I was wondering what was in that safe. It had to be code books or valuables."

Scowling, Dooley dragged his pack closer with his

feet, and scuffed it beneath his seat. "Bloody clever arse."

"When I first joined this group, you and the girl, you wanted to kill me . . ."

"Andrea still does, I still would given a suspicion of cause."

Boris hesitated before asking another question. "Does your hatred go so deep, will nothing ever sate it? When the war ends, or when every Communist, perhaps every Russian is dead, what then?"

"The ending of the war would make no difference." Clarence knew the answer, it dominated his waking thoughts, filled his dreams. "If it happened tomorrow I would find a way to go on. But it will not, will it? And I don't want the death of every Russian, I don't care if they are all killed, but I do not especially want it. All I want is six hundred to fall to me, two hundred for each of my family. I am over a third of the way towards that target."

It was the calm manner in which the words were spoken that struck Boris. "And when you reach that figure?"

"Most of my hunting is done in the Zone. The average life expectancy for a sniper is three weeks. I've been around fifteen months. I do not think it very likely I will have to make that decision."

HEADQUARTERS. AIR DEFENCE COMMAND. CENTRAL SECTOR. ZONE.

"I want them alive." General Pakovski picked up a chair and sent it crashing into a wall map. "Do you understand?"

The colonel had seen Pakovski in this mood before, and was frightened. "Of course, Comrade General. Everything will . . . is being done. We are getting reports . . ."

"Reports?" Pakovski's voice rose to a howl and he swept the contents of a bookcase to the floor. "I don't want reports, I want results. This tanker driver you mentioned, where is he?"

"Dead, Comrade General. They killed him."

"A pity. I would have done it. What of the civilians who were found nearby?"

"They have been questioned, but it is obvious they knew nothing."

"Shoot them; and the commander of the camp guard, and the guards at the bridge . . ." He paused. "Have I missed anyone?"

"No, Comrade General. There is this, Comrade General." The colonel offered a radio message pad.

"Read it."

"Yes, Comrade General. We are getting reports, garbled as yet, from a Frontal Aviation Staff Training Centre, south of Schonebeck. It would seem to be a sighting, but it is unconfirmed as yet."

"Then have it confirmed, and return when you have. This matter is important to me." Pakovski closed a hairy-backed hand around a jar of pencils and crushed it flat, splintering every one. "Remember, I want them alive. I want to deal with them myself." He let the fragments fall to the floor, where he crushed them under his boot.

NINE

From the cover of the wall, Libby could see the never-ending series of dashes of yellow light from the masked headlamps of the Russian and East German supply convoys. They had been moving along the road all night without a break.

He felt ill, the sick-giddy feeling that came with being over-tired. The damp cold did not help. It should have been possible to see the first faint lightening of the eastern horizon by now, but after hours of darkness unrelieved by moonlight, the dawn was being denied him by the growing mist forming over every watercourse and field.

The chilling water-particle laden air struck at him through the old horse blanket he had wrapped about himself and numbed him to the bone.

"Here, have this."

Libby took the coffee Ripper offered and hunched about it to draw its last drop of warmth. At the first sip he felt better, and had to force himself not to gulp it down immediately. Taking his time, he savoured every last drop and felt its warming effect radiate through his cold body.

"Traffic's thinning. Major says we'll be on our way again, soon as the flow is down to normal day time levels. You don't see much civvy traffic anytime, do you?"

"When the Warsaw Pact armies have finished pinching all the food, and every factory has been turned over to producing armaments, there's not enough left for the civilian population to be worth shifting about the country."

"What do they live on then?" Wisps of musty straw poked from beneath his jacket as Ripper beat his arms across his body.

"A lot of them don't, those that do, survive by growing their own food, or steal it, or play the black market."

"Jesus, what a way to live."

"You call that living?" Finishing the last dregs of the drink, Libby up-ended the cup to drain the semi-liquid residue of sugar.

The mist was growing thicker and the road was no longer visible. It was becoming lighter, but in a strangely luminous way, with no discernible source of illumination, as if the gods were making fractional adjustments on a giant dimmer switch.

"Almost like home." Ripper took deep breaths, as though savouring the dew-laden air. "After a start like this, I always found a day was good for hunting."

"Let's hope that doesn't hold true for the Russians today." Libby saw that the American now stood surrounded by mould-speckled shreds of hay and straw. "Is there a good reason for you to turn yourself

110

into an animated haystack?''

"Sure is. While you all been trying to keep your teeth from chattering, I've been as snug as a bug in a dung heap . . .''

"Smell like one as well.''

Ripper ignored the rude interruption, ". . . and you could, with some of this tucked all around you.'' He pulled out stalks from his sleeves and the top of his pants. "Kinda tickles down there, especially if you're not too careful and put a field mouse in as well. There's other problems too. I used to take my girl to her grandpa's barn, but after things went wrong a couple of times she didn't want to know. First time she got herself all smothered in corn husks: I goes in fast like I always does, and it were like screwing glasspaper. Still managed to finish but by then I was sore as hell, real raw.''

"That's quite a fund of little stories you've got. Are they all that poignant?''

It took Ripper a moment to recover from the shock of seeing the sergeant suddenly loom out of the mist. His fire-damaged face took on a spectral quality against the slowly swirling white backdrop.

"You ain't heard the half of this one yet. A couple of weeks and two tubes of antiseptic cream later we go back for another go. Maybe I'm the sort who doesn't learn by his mistakes, anyway I was all worked up and in a hurry again and I got real careless. You know what a head of barley looks like?''

"Why, you decided to change tack to a lecture on subsistence farming?''

"I'll tell you, it's hard, real hard, with lots of long sharp whiskery bits.'' Ripper wasn't about to be

111

deterred from the recounting of the episode. "Well, one of them critters got in the way. Damned near speared my foreskin and stabbed poor Barby right where it hurts."

"You finished?"

"No, Sarge, I recovered the full use of it inside of a week . . ."

"Just get aboard will you. We're moving. And get rid of that bloody straw. You look like something out of the Wizard of Oz."

Libby trailed behind the pair, watching Hyde help the Yank remove his insulation lagging. Now they were on their way again the tiredness wouldn't bother him, it would still be there, but the pressures and dangers would sublimate it to the need to stay alert. And there was another reason. They were driving back towards the Zone, would reach it today if luck was with them. The Zone meant refugees, and he would want to see everyone he could. To miss one might be to miss Helga. His war, his part in this war, would end the instant he found her.

The young Russian conscript manning the checkpoint barricade had gone a bleached white, and the clipboard in his hand was shaking visibly.

There had been no chance to avoid it. After rounding a bend in the fog it had loomed up immediately in front of them, and Burke had been forced to brake hard to avoid ramming the big counterweighted "H" beam blocking their path.

From the small guard hut came a bellow of

raucous laughter, and an empty bottle arched from the open doorway to smash at the edge of the road.

About two seconds that was how long the conscript had to live if he shouted a warning to his comrades loafing over the half-seen card table in the shack. His eyes flickered from the turret machine gun to the several tips of barrels that poked from various weapon ports. Every one was pointed at him.

Very slowly the fresh-faced youngster backed to the concrete block at the pole's end and put his weight on it. As it went down, the massive beam beyond the pivot rose from the supporting cradle on the far side of the road, and began to rise. Hunched over the rough-surfaced counterweight, the Russian closed his eyes tight, as though in prayer, and didn't look up as the eight-wheeler trundled past.

"Boris and Cline must be guessing right about those coded radio signals we keep intercepting. They're about us." Hyde knelt behind Revell's seat. "Perhaps we should be looking for a change of transport?"

"There's no need, not yet." Revell checked his map, pencilled in the location of the roadblock. "That kid won't have reported us, so as far as the Ruskies are concerned they'll think we're still back there, somewhere."

"And pretty soon they're going to realise we've slipped through. Better to make the switch now, while we've the chance to choose the time and place."

"I say stick with this wagon for as long as we can." Burke was enjoying the drive. The mist had lifted sufficiently for him to motor as close to the vehicle's top road speed as the twisting route would allow; enabling him to take advantage of the absence of other traffic, in the lull of activity between the resupply convoys using the cover of the dark, and the coming of full day, when civilian, inter-unit and local traffic would take over. "Where the hell would we get another Commie vehicle in this condition!"

Both driver and NCO had made good points, but for Revell it was a third argument that prompted his decision to press on as fast as they could. In fact it wasn't even an argument, it was a solid gut feeling that told him to go for mileage first and subtlety afterwards, but it would do no harm to offer a placatory gesture to the sergeant.

"Let's see if we can't have the best of both worlds. First chance we get we'll pull over and do what we can do to alter this APC's appearance. It's too distinctive, so let's see how we can make it look the same as the other Warsaw Pact wrecks of its type. God knows there's enough of them about, we should be able to merge into them. They can't possibly check every one."

As if to bear out Burke's argument, they passed three trucks pulled into the edge. Engine covers were raised on all three, as they were on a massive six-wheeled recovery vehicle a few hundred yards further on.

"We're being followed." Head poking out of an open hatch to catch some air and overcome the feeling of nausea the vehicle's harsh ride gave rise to, Cline had seen a pair of machine gun armed motorcycle combinations and an armoured car gaining on them. Any doubts he had as to whether or not the APC was the subject of a pursuit were swiftly dispelled when a roof-mounted klaxon on the car began to blare up and down the scale.

"Slow up. Let them get close." Revell tapped a grenade at Dooley's belt. "You and Andrea pitch them some presents. Half a dozen should do it."

The lead motorcycle had closed to twenty-five yards when the APC's side hatches were thrown open and the grenades tossed out.

Six irregular-shaped lumps of cast metal bounced on the road surface and rolled to a stop at its edge, then shattered and hurled fragments of metal in every direction.

Caught in the centre of the storm, the second combination disappeared from sight completely, hidden by the smoke and barely glimpsed flame of the detonations. The passenger and rider of the leading machine hunched low as they felt and heard the explosions behind them but it was too late. The bike's rear wheel deflated, slashed open by a sliver of casing, and at that instant the rider slumped over his handlebars, a gaping wound in his neck.

Making a wild grab for the controls the passenger attempted to avert disaster, but it was already inevitable. The bike's front wheel crabbed to the left and as the scuffing rubber sent it out of balance, men and machine were sent cartwheeling into the hedge.

As the mushroom of smoke from the grenades drifted upwards they were supplemented by a growing pall from the pools of blazing petrol and the burning bodies in the road. The armoured car had stopped, a front tyre fiercely alight. When the crew made a hurried exit to tackle the problem, Libby added to their discomfort with three short bursts he got off before a bend took them from sight. He thought he had missed, most of the tracer going high, until at the last moment he saw a crewman drop the extinguisher he was ineffectually wielding and clutch his stomach as he started to collapse.

"Cat's out of the bag now." Through a gap in the hedge Burke glimpsed witnesses to the incident.

Beside a netting-shrouded radio van stood several half-dressed East German signallers. Their open mouths made dark circles in their lathered faces.

"I reckon those guys are going to be telling tales inside of the next few minutes." The target the van presented was visible for too short a space of time for Ripper to get in a shot, and he heard others swearing at the missed opportunity.

"And a couple more after that, we are going to be the centre of a lot of attention." Cline checked that his rifle was within reach and patted his spare magazines. "If we get back we'll be able to tell them we took on a whole Russian army."

"And their airforce." Boris eased off the headphones. "Whoever is in charge of this search is pulling a lot of strings. Inter-service co-operation is not the Warsaw Pact's strongest point. Can we not use our radio to summon help of our own?"

"Not yet." Every few minutes Revell was trying to fix their position, keeping a constant update on their distance from the Zone. "The raid on Kothen was the first time NATO has made a deliberate incursion

116

into East Germany. If it's screwed up as bad as it sounds, then they're not going to be in a hurry to do it again. The longer we can hold out, the better chance we've got of getting some air-cover. Until then we're on our own, we sort out our own troubles."

"Got one for you now, Major." Burke pointed.

They were fast coming upon the tail-end of a long line of troops marching in single file down either side of the road. There seemed to be some confusion among them, particularly among those at the back. It was obvious they had heard the brief action, but being nearly twenty miles behind their own front line they didn't know what to make of it.

The first thing Revell noticed about them was that virtually every other man was carrying an anti-tank rocket launcher, and the second was that an NCO and an officer had stepped into the middle of the road to signal them to stop.

Burke didn't, and the officer paid dearly for his careless curiosity as he was struck by the trim board on the hull front and had his head almost severed from his body. The NCO moved quicker, but in the APC they felt the series of minor bumps as the wheels on one side passed over his legs.

Streams of tracer leapt from every port and cut down the lines of men before they even had a chance to unsling their weapons. From the turret Libby raked the road ahead, dissolving opposition before it could form.

Under the impact of the heavy bullets Libby saw heads burst like melons under a sledgehammer. He could hardly breathe in the poorly ventilated turret

117

and tears filled his eyes, but at such close range he could not miss. A few bullets hit the metal protecting him, but he hardly heard them above the noise of his machine gun, and he knew there was little chance of small-arms fire penetrating the most thickly armoured part of the APC.

Twice, the vehicle's gathering speed and the mount's limited depression, meant he couldn't bring the weapon to bear on small groups that hadn't panicked and looked like they might present a danger, but each time he saw the knot of soldiers disintegrate as the major used his assault shotgun.

When they reached the head of the column, Libby cranked furiously to turn the turret and then sent single shots or short bursts at any likely centre of retaliation. There were few.

In the space of twenty seconds a battalion-strength column had been reduced to a bloody shambles. Many soldiers had thrown down their weapons and run, hurling away their packs and other equipment as they fled across the fields. For two hundred yards the verges were littered with bodies. Sometimes it was just one, in other places four or five would be heaped upon each other and among them staggered or thrashed the maimed and dying.

Blood had splashed on Burke's vision block and he had to open the front port to be able to see where he was driving. The sudden rush of air helped to drive the stench of cordite from the interior. Hundreds of cartridge cases rolled on the floor, making an incessant clinking that grew irritating.

A dial on the panel caught his attention. It indicated over-heating in an engine. He reported it to Revell.

"Nurse it a bit further, but don't risk blowing it."

Andrea heard. She had used all her ammunition and had been about to help herself to some from Burke's pack. Taking three magazines she paused, then took a fourth. "It would not be a good time to start walking, would it?"

TEN

The trap had been hastily prepared but well sited. A tank transporter, still with its gutted T84 load aboard its semi-trailer, straddled the road. In the fields to either side Russian infantry had hurriedly dug-in, the ramparts of freshly turned earth betraying every position. Further back, a pair of BMP infantry combat vehicles were half-hidden hull-down in a fold.

"Through them or round them, Major?" Burke closed his port, forced to accept the stain-restricted visibility, knowing that to leave it open would have been to invite a storm of small-arms fire.

"Can't risk the damage of a collision. Let's take the scenic route."

At extreme range a hail of automatic fire struck the side of the APC as it turned off the road, crushing a rusted tubular steel gate into the soft earth. Great lumps of turf and loam smacked on the roof of hull and turret as shots from the BMP's 73mm guns added their weight. An RPG-7 anti-tank rocket flashed past, another self-destructed overhead and deep dents appeared in vulnerably thin top plates as most of that surface's paint was charred away or blistered by the fireball.

Libby sent retaliatory fire at the enemy infantry but without noticeable effect, the fields soaking up the tracer that didn't ricochet wildly into the sky. Even using all his skill and strength, he couldn't hold the unstabilised weapon steady for more than a couple of seconds at a time, against the savage bucking of the ride.

The BMPs started from concealment, pluming grey exhaust. Burke saw them and began to cut back towards the road. On the rough terrain the wheeled vehicle was at a disadvantage against its tracked opponents, whose better cross-country performance was already enabling them to close the gap as they took short cuts through patches of ground that Burke had to avoid for fear of bogging down.

A 73mm shell blasted a crater in the meadow fifty yards to their left, and shortly afterwards a second impacted against a tree even further off. Libby watched the guns on both BMPs go to maximum elevation immediately, as they had to in order for the breeches to be aligned with the feeding ramp of the semi-automatic loaders. That added the problem of re-sighting the unstabilised gun after every shot to the Russian gunners' other problems in their severely cramped turrets and slowed their rate of fire to once a minute at most.

Libby kept watch on the lead vehicle, and as its smooth-bore gun depressed to the horizontal called a warning to their driver. The violent course correction was hardly needed, as two more shells fell little nearer than the first. And then the APC thundered back on to the metalled surface of the road and, picking up speed, began to pull away from its pursuers.

Almost the instant they reached top speed, an engine began to misfire, and Burke could no longer ignore the temperature gauge beginning to push into the red.

"What now, Major?" Hyde had been reading the map over the officer's shoulder. "No turnings off this road, and we can't lose those Ruskies by outpacing them. Could be we'll be thinking on our feet again soon."

"How long we'll be stood on them is what bothers me. At my best pace a BMP can catch me in bottom gear." By slowing Burke had managed to keep the tell-tale needle hovering just short of the danger point, but even that was not enough. At that temperature the coolant would soon be boiled away and when the engine seized there would be no point in trying to continue on the remaining one. Its ninety horsepower would be insufficient to hold their lead, and the moment they hit a serious gradient the APC would be slowed to a crawl. Then with the enemy machines closing fast it would be no better than a barely mobile crematorium, for the impact of the first high explosive anti-tank shell would turn it into a pyre.

To underline his thoughts a round crashed into the road behind them, and another scorched past, carrying away a headlamp and setting ablaze a truck parked further on.

An oncoming ambulance convoy scattered as shells followed the APC's swerving progress. A cross-marked Tatra fell apart as it was side-swiped by the lead BMP, turning over into the ditch and spilling its bandaged occupants into the stagnant water amid a tangle of drip-feeds and broken stretchers.

Aiming straight back down the road, Libby saw his tracer bounce from the sharp raked front of the BMPs without effect. The range was down to four hundred yards and on the smoother surface the Russian gunners had improved their rate of fire. Still not accurate, the weight of fire would eventually tell. Libby knew that his chances of getting out were so slim as to be non-existent.

If the hit was on the turret then he would never know about it. Capable of punching through a hundred millimetres of armour, the turret's fourteen would provide no impediment to the shell's tungsten tip. And at the moment of penetration the round's explosive filling would destroy the turret, very likely setting off the fuel and ammunition, and accounting for most of the others as well. But if the hit were elsewhere, perhaps on the engines, or through the side of the hull, then the interior would be flooded with fire and, trapped in his seat, he would suffer the most terrible of deaths, being burnt alive.

Three hundred yards, and now the shells were falling so close they rocked the vehicle. Fragments of casing hammered the armour, the tip of one piece piercing the turret wall and sending sparks into the side of Libby's face.

Above the roar of another near-miss he heard a scream, too high-pitched for a man: Andrea had been hit. Keeping the machine gun firing until the barrel smoked, Libby sent an endless line of bullets at the Russian driver's vision slits, and saw the leader skid and almost cause a collision before control was regained.

When it was the gap had opened again, and stayed open.

Towing swirling steam, the APC reached the outskirts of a village. Better kept than many they had passed, they raced into it along its single main street, and were close to its centre when Revell saw what lay ahead.

Heavily armed KGB troops were pushing and herding civilians into the road so that they filled it from the buildings on one side to the other. As Revell spotted them the Russians, with kicks and threats, began to force the people to the ground.

At forty miles an hour the APC was driving straight at a human roadblock. Having traversed forward at the officer's shout Libby sent a long burst over the civilians' heads. A couple jumped to their feet, and were felled by shots from KGB machine pistols. The others stayed down, and Libby saw them closing their eyes and hugging each other in small family groups.

Down to twenty miles an hour, the terrified people only yards ahead and the BMPs closing fast, Burke looked for a side turning and saw none. The front wheels were almost upon an elderly couple when he threw the steering hard over and sent the APC ploughing into a shop front.

Its mass carried it through the windows and splintered the counters, crushing the pathetically few goods on display, and then it struck the rear wall and a deluge of debris rained down.

The wheels spun on the loose rubble, then Burke shifted down into the lowest gear and the APC began to grind forward, climbing the heap of rubble that had been the back wall. It thumped down into the brick-strewn back garden as the roof caved in, leaving only the shell of the building standing.

A succession of fences collapsed before the APC, then it swerved back on to the road, taking away the corner of a house as it negotiated a narrow alleyway to do so.

Knowing there was a possibility of a breech explosion if the barrel had become blocked or bent, Libby tried a single shot, then a short burst when that proved safe. He forced his aching arm to work the traverse mechanism and had a clear view of the road just as the Russian vehicles reached the civilians.

Minds numbed by the threats and violence, most of them still sat or stood in the road. The BMPs didn't stop, didn't even slacken speed.

"They're driving through them . . . there's kids there." To Libby it looked deliberate when the second BMP made a separate lane of its own through the East Germans. "Get them, get the bastards."

Burke hurled the eight-wheeler through a turn that put it in behind a whitewashed greenhouse beside the road, as the leading vehicle raced past.

At point-blank range Libby put fifty rounds of armour-piercing and incendiary into the BMP's bulbous rear doors. Jets of fuel hosed the road in its wake, then became tongues of bright flame. Out of control, gouting fire from every hatch and vent and port, the vehicle jerked and bucked and swerved until, hitting steep steps at the front of a house, it canted over and toppled on to its side, tracks still thrashing round in the centre of a growing lake of blazing fuel.

The greenhouse shattered as the APC charged through it and rammed the second BMP amidships. Whipping lengths of track ripped away sections of the enemy vehicle's thin aluminum track covers as it was broken by the pounding impact.

Applying full power, able to see only the two-tone grey side of the BMP, Burke pushed the crippled vehicle across the road into the corner of a house. The substantial stone structure resisted the charge and the APC was backed off to repeat the tactic.

Crewmen were struggling to escape through buckled hatches when the APC struck again, and were hurled back inside by the avalanche of masonry that came down as the wall collapsed to bury them and their transport.

"Hold it." Libby came down from his seat as Burke began to turn the APC on to its original heading. "We're not leaving."

"Don't be damned stupid." Temporarily trapped by loose equipment the collisions had piled about him, Revell could only twist round in his seat to confront the armourer. "Reinforcements could be here any moment."

"I'm with Libby." From his weapon port Clarence could see the remains of the civilians. "Leave us if you like, but we have a score to settle with half a dozen KGB thugs."

"And I stay also." There was a livid brown scar on

127

Andrea's cheek, where a red-hot fragment had struck. The area around it was heavily bruised and there was blood at the corner of her mouth.

"Then we'd better deal with them quick as we can." Pushing aside the last of the packs, Revell stood and reached for his hatch lock. "Well, come on then."

Leaving the APC unattended they sprinted along the side of the street until they reached the stomach-wrenching site of the slaughter. Most of those mowed down had been killed immediately, but a few clung to life. Among them a pregnant woman whose left leg had been crushed to a bloody pulp; and worse, a child, perhaps ten years old, a pretty blonde girl whose face was now distorted with suffering as she lay with her back broken in the middle of the road.

Clarence went over to her, despite attempts by others to hold him back. As he reached her and bent to lift her slight frame a shot rang out and a bullet aimed for him missed and finished the girl's suffering.

Two bellows blended as one. Side by side Clarence and Libby raced for the building, while a fusillade of fire from the others gave them cover.

Hitting the door first, the sniper shoulder-charged through it, and as he went sprawling Libby fired over him to bring down the Russian who had just reached the bottom of the stairs.

Jagged bone protruded from the KGB man's shattered leg, but he still managed to snarl at Libby before his mouth was ruined by a savage blow with a rifle butt. Again and again the weapon was driven down with pile-driver force, joined by a second as

128

Clarence caught up.

Hearing a back door slam they ran through the house, and had to duck back as bullets gouged into the doorpost and lintel.

Libby had glimpsed a field car being hastily boarded by several Russians, and when he and Clarence appeared at the opening again it was to hurl grenades.

When they looked up only one man was still at the vehicle. Hands tight-locked on the steering wheel, the driver stared rigidly ahead, oblivious of the fire on the back seat. Blood spurted from a hole in the side of his head, then slowed to a trickle, then stopped as he fell forward.

Two others lay dead, but a third, a captain, had only been dazed by the blast and as he shook himself back to full consciousness the first thing he saw was the barrels of two rifles.

He screamed as his elbows were smashed, then without stopping shrieked louder still as more bullets did the same to his kneecaps. His agony ended abruptly as his heart failed and he vomited blood, went blue in the face and died.

"I hate the Communists for what they are doing to me." Turning away from the body, it was an automatic action for Clarence to reload his Enfield Enforcer.

Taking a last look at the Russian officer, Libby trailed behind the sniper. "I hate them for what they're doing to everyone."

"Any luck?" Hyde joined their radio operators.

"Luck doesn't enter into it, Sarge, this is skill I'm using." Cline winced as loud static assaulted his ears.

"Well, is your skill getting us anywhere then?"

"Eh, not yet." Thinking to salvage something of his self-proclaimed reputation, Cline added, "It's this Russian equipment, we can't use it to broadcast because it's incompatible with the Jaguar sets NATO uses, and it's hoping for a bit much to expect our radio intercept units to monitor it by chance."

"So what are you tinkering about with?"

Cline held up their man-pack radio. "We're, I'm," seeing no reason to share any laurels, Cline changed from the plural to the singular, "using the Ruskie equipment to boost this thing's short-range."

"A combination of British brains and Russian brawn, I like it. OK, keep at it." Hyde hauled himself from the vehicle, and joined Revell at the edge of the copse in which they'd concealed the APC. "Quite a view, Major." He ducked into the undergrowth and accepted the field glasses from the officer.

On the NATO side the Zone tended to peter out, with only the insubstantial barbed wire fences to mark its boundary, but on the Soviet side it was precisely and starkly marked by the old Iron Curtain; the snaking tract of wire and steel and concrete that had separated East Germany from the Free World in pre-war days. The walls and towers and some of the tank obstacles were still visible, but the ploughed strip to either side had long been overgrown, though beneath the breeze-swayed grass, flecked with the first spring flowers, still nestled the anti-personnel mines and man-traps. Once denuded of trees, even the first of those was making a comeback and the pliant young trunks hid some of the directional mine-topped stakes that had been the last cruel innovation, before the Russian armies had swept into West Germany and made them obsolete.

"You said this was a quiet sector, Major." Hyde panned the glasses from one enemy concentration to the next, "I'm glad we're not going to be busting through one of the busy ones."

"I'll admit it looks a lot, but look again. Most of the vehicles are softskins and the camps are for the pioneers working all the dumps you can see."

"That's still a lot of Ruskies. There's only one road through the minefields and the wall and it's blocked to traffic." Adjusting the focus, Hyde concentrated his attention on a checkpoint where the road passed an observation tower.

Apart from a dozen or more armed military police and a couple of scout cars, a troop of T62s sat at the foot of the ribbed concrete column.

As he watched, Hyde saw the troops swarm about an eight-wheel APC that had halted at the barricade. A T62 nudged forward, its cannon aimed at the vehicle's hull front. The crew were rousted out and searched, and their papers taken for examination at a nearby hut.

"It's for certain we won't be able to force our way through that, not as it stands now." Hyde returned the glasses.

Boris came up behind them. "Bombardier Cline's compliments, Major. He says he has established the link you required."

"Don't you want your share of the credit?"

A shake of the head and a small smile was Boris's

only reply.

Revell knew what the Russian was up to. The bombardier would be in his debt now, and in war if you can't have friends, people who owe you favours can be just as valuable. Boris was building up a stock.

While Cline made a great show of fussing about with minor and mostly unneeded adjustments, Revell put on the headset. The voice on the other end was instantly identifiable. He turned down the volume against the torrent of shouted obscenity, and even then had to hold the earphones away from his head.

"That's our colonel Lee J. Lippincott, Ol' Foul Mouth himself," Dooley offered to an astounded Cline, by way of explanation, as the bombardier's mouth dropped open on hearing the tirade come over the air. "He must be glad we're still alive, must be all choked up; he's usually a lot more fluent than that."

Hyde joined Dooley in craning forward to listen in. "Just wait 'til the major puts in our request. He'll soon regain his old form."

"Colonel . . . Colonel," Revell was having trouble breaking into the flow. "Yes, Colonel . . . Like you say, Colonel, I must be a real crafty fucker. Colonel . . . I want a sky strike . . ."

The swearing from the other end intensified fourfold and Revell was able to reduce the volume still further.

"He'll get us one." Dooley sat back, nodding sagely. "I know Ol' Foul Mouth, he'd have got nasty if he weren't going to do it."

Listening to the language being used, Cline couldn't understand how Dooley knew that their commanding officer hadn't turned nasty. He asked.

"That? That's nothing. When the colonel gets into his stride he can go on for twenty minutes without repeating himself, but with him what you've got to watch out for is when he stops cussing. Then he gets really dangerous. If he ever smiles at you and says a polite good-morning, you might as well go back and shoot yourself." Dooley leant close again to catch a few words. "Oh yeah, we're getting our sky strike, he's still going strong . . ."

ELEVEN

"They want us to mark the target. What have we got?"

"Nothing with the range to do it from here." Hyde was already aware of the airforce's requirement, and had been working on it. "The three closest dumps are the best part of fifteen hundred yards off. We could hit them with the turret machine gun, but there's not much chance of starting fires at that sort of range. What it needs is a grenade or two plonked into the middle of each one."

Andrea pushed between the officer and NCO.

"From the bottom of the hill I could hit them with this."

She held up her grenade-launcher-fitted M16. Her words were slightly slurred as she tried to talk with her damaged mouth.

He really did admire her, Revell just couldn't help it. Even the puffiness of her face around the injured cheek couldn't detract from her basic beauty, and her determination clearly came through her painful impediment.

It was more than admiration though, perhaps not love yet, desire definitely, but not love. But the word love was always one that figured in his thinking about her.

"Well, do I go?"

Her piercing blue eyes were on him, startlingly pale when the sun was directly on her face, adding to her intensity of expression. He didn't like her being away from him, but couldn't deny she was the best they had with that weapon and could do the job if anyone could. Someone would have to go with her, to give supporting fire if she was spotted. If only it could be him, but it couldn't be. He felt he was making himself obvious as it was. No, if there had to be another with her then he'd pick a man he could trust . . .

They slipped and slid on the damp grass of the steep hillside from one patch of sharp-needled hawthorn to the next. Being lighter and nimbler, Andrea set a fast pace for each sprint, and Libby had to work hard to keep up.

"This will do." Libby drew the girl into a thicket where the white flowered bushes were mixed with ivy-draped stunted oaks.

"It is not close enough." She made to go on. "We are at the weapon's maximum range."

Keeping hold of her arm, Libby pulled her to the ground behind a toppled oak. "If we go any lower we won't be able to see the targets as clearly, or observe our fall of shot."

Andrea said nothing, but signalled her acceptance of the argument by unslinging her depleted bag of rifle grenades. She pushed three explosive rounds into Libby's hand. "Hold these, set them for impact detonation."

"As you ask so nicely, certainly."

For a couple of minutes they worked in silence, using the edges of coins to dial the correct settings on the nosetips of the fuses.

"Do you really still expect to find your girlfriend?"

Coming out of the blue, her words caught Libby totally unprepared, and astounded him. He had never exchanged more than a few dozen words with Andrea, and all those had been essential, in action. Until now he hadn't even realised she knew anything about him, she had never shown any interest.

"My fiancée? Yes, I'll find her." That was the first time he had ever said the words out loud. Their sound did not reflect the confidence he'd always felt he had. He sought to reinforce them. "Of course I will, it's just a matter of time."

"It has become an obsession, yes?"

That wasn't so easy to answer. His immediate reaction was an honest, spontaneous "yes," but he curbed it. In a sense his quest had become an obsession, but its cause was still the same as it had always been, to restore to him the one person who meant something to him, who had meant everything, who still did.

"You might think so."

"But you do not." Andrea toyed with an armed grenade, looking at but not seeing its colour-coded body. "To you it is much more than that, but the words do not come easily. It is love?"

"More than you could ever comprehend." These were things Libby had never talked of with anyone before. Even with Helga he'd become tongue-tied on the subject, and a thousand million times since the start of the war he'd wished he'd said to her more often what was in his heart. And now he was talking about it with a hard-faced East German bitch who used and discarded men like she might a paper handkerchief, with no more thought.

Andrea slowly loaded the launcher. "In that you are right. I cannot comprehend what it is like to have a man so devoted, so dedicated . . ."

"What? You could have any man you wanted."

"Could I have you? No, I do not mean it that way, but perhaps you see what I mean. A woman does not want any man, no more than a real man wants every woman."

"Is it that you don't like men?" Libby tentatively, and in a roundabout way, put the question that most members of the squad had speculated on at some time.

"Why not ask the question directly. What you want to know is do I like women. It is not a question I can answer yes or no. I have loved a woman, a girl, but it was a long time ago and it was not a physical relationship. Does that disappoint you, were you hoping for details?"

Libby hadn't, but couldn't find the form of words to express what it was he'd really meant to say. Reaching out, he put a finger lightly on her injured face. "Does it hurt much?" In the manner in which she'd repelled advances from others, Libby had expected her to knock his hand away, but she didn't, allowing him to run his finger down her cheek, skirting the bruising, to reach and pause, still touching, at the corner of her mouth. With Helga he'd been able to convey his feelings more often by a caress, than by words.

"My cheekbone may be broken, a tooth has been loosened and another is sharp: yes it hurts, but I can bear it. I can still do my work."

"How come you're talking to me now, what's changed?"

"Nothing has changed, yet I . . . I have a feeling . . . that you will not be with us for much longer . . . I felt I could talk to you . . ."

"Because I won't be about to blab it to others. Thanks."

"You can think that if you wish."

She turned her back on him and didn't speak again. He almost grabbed her and asked her what she meant when she said he wouldn't be with the squad for much longer, but didn't. Damn it, he was as superstitious as the next bloke, but that was taking it a bit far. Stupid, there couldn't be anything in it . . . couldn't be.

"The party starts in ten minutes." Revell turned the glasses towards the nearest dumps. "Andrea should be doing her bit right about . . . now."

From the foot of the slope came the muted crump of a grenade thrower, and a second later there was a burst of flame close to the perimeter of an area littered with stacks of wooden crates. A mushroom of smoke that rose in the cool air was swiftly dispersed in the freshening wind.

Another shot landed dead centre among a park of handling equipment just beside a guard hut. The smoke cleared to reveal the flimsy structure swaying in the breeze with its end wall collapsed. A forklift truck had been overturned, but there was no sign of the hoped for conflagration.

"Shift target, girl. Shift target."

As though she could hear him, the third grenade detonated among a group of Russian pioneers seeking shelter beneath a tracked ammunition carrier. Cases of shells close by were pushed over by the blast and spilled their contents, but there was no chain-reaction in the ammunition dump.

Revell heard the fourth shot fired, but there was no following explosion, and he cursed the faulty fuse. Now he switched his attention to the only other target within range of Andrea's launcher. Of the three it had looked the least promising, just a few stacks of boxes that rated only a bare three-strand barbed wire fence, and that unlike the other depots off the main road didn't even warrant a guard on its entrance.

Number five was as disappointing as the earlier attempts, being just too long, and falling over the far side of the dump and blasting an unoffending shed that disintegrated without a single splinter taking flame.

The ground between the foot of the hill and the wall was like a seething ants' nest viewed from above. Pioneers and construction troops were rushing about to find cover and fighting each other when any place

140

of imagined safety was found. What had been a fairly orderly forward staging area was now a confused mass of panicking Russians.

Striking a patch of clear ground in an obscure corner of the third dump, Andrea's last grenade looked to be even less successful than those that had gone before, but as the dirt settled back and the last wisps of smoke were whirled away and lost, a pillar of fire leapt from the shallow crater.

"No bloody wonder they weren't bothering to guard the place." Hyde watched the tall gout of flame turn to a spitting fountain that spawned a mass of other fires. Another underground storage tank was ignited and consumed in a single giant bubble of red and yellow that soared upwards. "Even Dooley wouldn't try to pinch napalm."

"Kinda looks like you got your target marker, Major, and with time to spare. Planes ain't due for another five minutes yet." Ripper was enjoying the spectacle. A sharp prod in the back from Hyde dissuaded him from repeating the rebel yell with which he had greeted the first fiery eruption.

"And it also looks as if Libby and Andrea have been spotted." Using the powerful telescope on his rifle, Clarence kept track of the T62 that was moving towards the hill. The tank's co-axial machine gun was already in action and now the main armament commenced a slow rate of fire, its shot landing among the belt of dense trees and undergrowth a little above the foot of the slope.

"In the APC, and draw their fire." Much of the effect of the T62's shooting could not be seen, but now and again a high explosive round would burst among the tops of the trees and lengths of smoulder-ing bough and bark and trunk would sail spinning through the air.

Revell only knew the pair's approximate position, but he could see the shells falling all about it and his mouth went so dry he found it hard to catch a breath.

The vehicle's turret machine gun clattered loudly and sent a line of tracer at the advancing tank. A second followed, then another: and then Revell saw its cannon traverse towards them and elevate.

A solid shot struck the hill lower down, the following high explosive round came no nearer.

"They can't elevate enough." Hyde could imagine the Russian commander's frustration, then saw it demonstrated as the man brought the tank's anti-aircraft machine gun into play.

Already having the range, it was an opportunity Clarence did not neglect. He fired twice, short bursts whose arcing trajectory was marked by dashes of bright green tracer. Before the tank man could settle behind his weapon he was hit, threw up his arms and collapsed to drape his upper torso over the side of the turret.

Burke didn't hear the Harriers' approach. One moment the sky was clear save for the thick column of smoke from the dump, the next they were hurtling at zero feet over the wall, unleashing salvo after salvo of 68mm air to ground rockets from their underwing Matra pods.

The effect was devastating. Traffic that wasn't blasted off the road collided with the blazing debris, as truck and transporter drivers abandoned their still-rolling vehicles. A carpet of destruction preceded the jets as they swept over the area.

All four aircraft banked to scream past the hill in succession, so close that Revell could see the pilots and feel the buffeting effect of their slipstream and the pungent heat of their exhausts.

The second pass was more selective and saturation tactics gave way to precision bombardment. Both T62s were singled out and in turn were pounded by direct hits that reduced both to burning hulks. The scout cars, checkpoint and watch tower received the same attention. Several rockets fell into the minefield and initiated a chain-reaction, while still others blasted holes in the wall.

Among the inferno of devastation, individuals and groups of Russians ran from place to place seeking shelter from the howling flame-tailed warheads, but there was nowhere to go and many were cut down as they ran or threw themselves into some imagined place of safety, only for it to be obliterated by a direct hit.

They were gone as quickly as they had come, using their unique vectoring ability to execute impossibly tight turns at the end of their second run to set them on their course for home.

In that short space of time, not more than half a minute from their appearance to their departure, the Harriers had pulverized the area of the wall and its defences, and wrought bloody havoc among the troops and dumps flanking the road.

There was no need to order the others to board, when Revell reached for the grabrail on the side of the APC he was the last to do so. Burke was tackling the, in places, near-sheer decline even before he was

143

in his seat.

Even when at times he locked all the wheels, their driver could not prevent their transport gathering speed. In desperation, as it threatened to run out of control, he deliberately steered it through the clumps of coarse growth dotting the slope and as, one after another, the tough twisted trunks of hawthorns resisted before yielding to the vehicle's progress, its headlong career was checked, and its speed reduced to a level where he at least had the chance of maintaining some degree of control.

Revell stood peering out of the open hatch as they neared the place from which the grenades had been launched, searching the cratered terrain for Andrea and Libby.

The air still held a strong smell of cordite, now being reinforced and at times swamped by the stink from the many fires among the tussocks of spark-generating grass and felled trees. To them was added the smoke and stench of the fires among the dumps, and together the pall was being thickened to a state that compared with the fog they'd endured around dawn.

When he saw them, Revell found his thoughts and emotions crowding him with conflict. She seemed unharmed, and at that realization he felt exaltation. Then he saw Libby extend his hand to her, to assist her over a tangle of fallen wood, and saw her take it, without hesitation.

Seeing it made him think of his ex-wife, of how the cold cow had eventually come to reject the physical aspects of their marriage, how in the last six months before they'd separated she'd never once let him touch her. And then he remembered how he'd felt on the day of their divorce, when she'd thrown at him the news that she was having an affair, and was already pregnant by a salesman she'd met only weeks before.

The turmoil in his mind at this moment was something like that. Andrea, with whom he'd never got anywhere, who was so untouchable and had frozen him out, being familiar with someone else. The sight brought him pain and anger and he had to struggle to keep the feelings from his voice when he called to urge them on.

Closed down tight, with every weapon port manned, they drove towards the fires, and as they steered between two blazing dumps, heading towards the road, a human tide of screaming Russian infantry rushed towards them.

TWELVE

Every single man was on fire. Some flapping at burning sleeves and jacket fronts as they ran, others were no more than animated balls of flame from which hands and feet projected.

Several of them deliberately threw themselves under the APC to put an end to their suffering and the suspension couldn't damp the jolting and bouncing as skulls and ribcages made unnatural obstacles for the wheels.

A few tried to cling to the hull, pounding with blistered fists at the armour as they begged for help, but most just ran, heads down with their teeth clenched and their jaws set in expressions of utter determination, as though they could win the race against the flames the draught spread over their bodies.

Those too severely injured to move sat, or lay, and waited for the tides of liquid fire to roll over them. Among the petrol fires ammunition dumps began to erratically explode and added a further ingredient to the boiling hell.

The hull of the APC was becoming too hot to touch, and there was a strong aroma of burning rubber as the tyres steamed in the roasting air.

Libby had climbed into the turret seat their sniper had vacated for him, but there were no targets. When the vehicle slewed on to the road there was no opposition, no living Russian in sight. Twice they had to bulldoze wrecks aside, but there was no other obstruction to their progress.

Bodies sprawled about two damaged scout cars and a knocked-out T62. A crudely painted black and white striped pole lay splintered at the roadside. Short lengths of barbed wire impaled the APC's tyres and were carried round several times before being dislodged, making scraping contact with the hull at each revolution.

"We've made it." Burke steered the vehicle around a chicane of tank obstacles and through the gap in the wall.

"Oh yeah, out of the frying pan . . ."

"Into the Zone." Hyde completed Dooley's sentence for him.

"Well at least the bloody roads won't be stiff with sodding Commies." Following the major's instructions, Burke took a right fork, then turned on to a narrow side road that barely admitted the nine-foot-wide eight-wheeler.

"Back there we could see the fuckers." Dooley jerked his thumb over his shoulder, towards East Germany. "This is the Zone, from now on we won't see sodding nobody until we drive into the middle of a Ruskie battlegroup, or an ambush by armed civvies."

"Hope not." After counting his spare magazines twice, Ripper replaced all three in his pouch. "We tackle anything more than a bunch of wild dogs and we is gonna be in real big trouble. Anybody else noticed we're getting a mite short on ammo?"

The APC frequently brushed both sides of the road at once. Grass and weeds were making a strong bid to reclaim the road and had already carpeted large patches. Every gate, every wall and abandoned farm was the object of an assault by nature. Winter might have imposed a temporary halt to the encroachment, but the first days of spring were bringing reinforcement and fresh vigour to the one-sided contest.

Only rarely were there any signs of the violent warfare that had ranged and raged across the fields and hills in the early days of the war. The most obvious were the occasional glimpses of rusting tanks and other armoured vehicles, and once, the tailplane of a Mig 21, suspended by the scorched branches of a giant elm, above a wide, shallow, water-filled crater, at the edge of which some of the tree's roots were exposed.

As they drove further in though, they began to come across more recent evidence of fighting, or of bombardment. Such an instance was the small town of Liebenburg. It had virtually ceased to exist.

On the outskirts a few buildings survived, most without roofs, and none with windows or doors, but as they drove further in, bricks and splintered window frames crunching under the wheels, there was less and less to see: less and less that was even recognisable as the remains of what had once been a prosperous and bustling town.

Ground zero of the nuclear demolition device was marked by the fused stump of a church tower, standing only a couple of feet high, with the runs of molten stone, now long solidified, radiating from it. Every tombstone of the graveyard that had flanked it on all sides echoed the star-like pattern, pressed down into the baked earth by the irresistible blast, their deep etched inscriptions wiped away by a heat greater than the heart of the sun that now glinted on the glassy slabs.

There seemed no reason for the destruction, the town had not lain in the path of any major axis of the first Soviet advances, no river or road or railway gave the place strategic or even tactical importance. Then as they drove out on the far side, they understood, and could only wonder at the courage, and the fate of the atomic demolition troops who had returned to the town after the first disorganised retreats and set the device that had inflicted such a blow on the Warsaw Pact armies.

In street after street, or where the streets had been, sat the rusting fire-ravaged bulks of Soviet missile launchers, more than they could count. Tracked launch and reload vehicles with their attendant mass of support equipment, even mobile radar units had been caught and now rested on their axles or padless tracks.

It was as the APC cleared the desolation of

Liebenburg that they saw the feather-like contrails, and were warned in time to change course.

Revell saw them first, and knew they weren't those of aircraft. The lines of vapour made three upright dashes in the clear sky, and each was hooked at its top, marking the apogee of each bombardment rocket's trajectory. He ordered their driver to pull over, and with the engines switched off, they waited.

Impact must have been all of five miles away, but the missile's conventional warheads delivered a crashing punch. Bright crescents flared over the hills, followed by the distinctive frosty-white haloes of blast waves. A short count later there came the crack and rolling boom of each explosion, one fast upon another.

"NATO Command doesn't drop Pershings on road repair gangs." From the rear hatch Libby watched the mushrooms of smoke soar upwards. Almost immediately they were chased by other darker clouds that could only come from burning fuel and ammunition. "Those three babies have stopped us from running into a Ruskie armoured regiment or battle group."

He dropped back down to let Boris and Cline take his place. The pair kept jostling each other for most room and the best position. The major had already taken a heading on the explosions, and was consulting his map.

"There's a decent route through here, Major." With his little finger Libby traced a path into the Harz nature park area. "Means striking south for a while, but we'll avoid whatever's ahead, and north is no alternative, that'll only take us towards the

Hanover salient. Things are still pretty hot up there, it'd be easy to drive into trouble."

"It could be that you have an interest in going south, could it?" Hyde had overheard the suggestion. "Wouldn't be because you know there's a few refugees that way, would it?"

Libby didn't respond, just watched the officer, intensely, as though by concentration of sheer willpower he could hope to influence his thinking. He hung on his words as he spoke.

"Whatever, it makes sense. We turn south."

Relief surged through Libby, though he didn't understand himself why the decision was so important to him. It was a feeling he had; no, not even as concrete a concept as that, it was just something inside him, telling him to go there.

At the sound of the engine starting, as they began to move and he returned to the turret, for the first time in two years he felt his spirits lifting, a heady almost drunken feeling. There was no way he could tell, nothing to go on, but he felt now he was drawing nearer to Helga. The sickeningly bumpy vehicle that he had come in two days to hate now seemed the sweetest, smoothest conveyance ever made. Taking him the way he wanted to go, he would not have complained, would hardly have noticed, if it'd been fitted with square wheels.

Now they were passing through an area that had repeatedly seen heavy fighting. No field was without its quota of abandoned Leopard, Chieftan, M60 or T84 tanks. Most had burned, and those that hadn't the engineers had destroyed.

From the first day this had been an unrelenting war of attrition, and as the fortunes of battle swept back and forth neither side had allowed the other to capture its vehicles, or recapture its own. If a tank was knocked out, then the special squads of either side raced to be first to reach it. What could not be immediately towed to the rear for repair was blasted apart. Battle damage or breakdown, it made no difference, all that mattered was that nothing salvable should be allowed to fall into enemy hands.

As the war had progressed the engineers of both sides had grown highly proficient, as the extravagantly twisted metalwork of the hulks testified.

And it wasn't only tanks that littered the fields and roadsides. For each knocked-out tank, three or four armoured personnel carriers and twenty or more softskin vehicles fell victim to close range attack, or missile or gun bombardment, or to the fighter-bomber and helicopter gunships.

In places where no one had bothered, or had time to deal with route clearance, long sections of highway were blocked by burned-out or overturned transport of every description. There were other indications also, of how fast and fluid the battles had been, and how the sites had not been visited since. Everywhere there were rag-garbed skeletons, in jeeps, draped from tank turrets, laid about guns and collapsed in the bottom of shallow slit-trenches. Only a few of the dead had found even the temporary haven of a roadside grave, and by one unnatural hummock lay several spade-clutching corpses in the last stages of decomposition. On the modern battle-

153

field it was dangerous, often lethal, to delay even long enough to bury a fallen comrade.

After a third nerve-racking halt to take on water for the overheating engine, Burke watched the temperature gauge needle climbing even more rapidly than before.

"If you don't let me stop, Major, and have a look for the trouble, then we are going to lose an engine. It's rough now, and burning oil, another ten miles and either something is going to melt or we're all going to fry. I've got the heater turned up full to circulate the water as much as possible, and I don't know about you, but I'm already to tuck up me toes with heat prostration."

"OK. I got a glimpse of a place from the top of that last hill. Should be around here somewhere." Revell scanned the seemingly never-ending vista of conifers to either side. "We'll pull in and have a look at the trouble."

"We might be lucky if we can do that." Easing back on the speed, Burke watched the needle inexorably rising into the red. "I've had a look inside a few Commie engine compartments. They weren't ever designed with maintenance in mind. I thought the early Chieftains were pigs to work on until I saw the guts of a T72. This bugger has two engines, and that ain't going to make it no easier."

They were almost past the small petrol station before they saw it, and Burke had to slam on the brakes and turn tightly to pull on to its forecourt. The doors to an advertisement-plastered corrugated iron workshop were open, and Burke drove staight in, parking the APC over an inspection pit.

"Where are you off to?"

Revell had spotted Dooley's unsuccessful attempt to make a hurried and quiet exit, something that his bulk and nature made nearly impossible.

"Thought I'd check the place over, Major, make sure there were no Ruskies around."

"More likely to see if there was anything worth pocketing." Enjoying the welcome sensation of stretching, after the long hours of confinement in the uncomfortable command seat, Revell gazed about the shed. From the look of the place it appeared unlikely that Dooley could find anything of value, even a large compartmented rack that must previously have held thousands of nuts, bolts and washers had been emptied, and not a single tool or grease gun was left on any of the illegibly labelled racks on the walls. "You want to play jackdaw, then check those two tool boxes on the roof of this wagon. If they're as lavishly equipped as the rest of it, we should be able to do anything short of a rebore or engine change."

Muttering under his breath, Dooley hauled himself on top of the APC. The boxes the officer had mentioned were non-standard additions, welded to the roof beside the escape hatch just forward of the engine compartment. Fabricated from mild steel sheet, they had suffered considerable damage.

One was already hanging open, its lid all but ripped away and the sides crushed to half their proper height. A few spanners and wrenches lay amongst the brick dust and broken masonry lining its bottom.

The other had not suffered so badly during their progress through the village store, but a large chunk of brick was wedged in a bent-back corner. It was also scorched, and a fragment of rocket casing had pierced and lodged in the lid.

Employing one of the wrenches, Dooley smashed its lock, and reached in to lift out its contents. "Look what I found. A new toy for Libby." He held up the launch tube of the shoulder-fired Grail anti-aircraft missile. "Think we'll find a use for it, Sarge?"

Hyde looked up from assisting Burke with the unfastening of the engine access panels. "I don't think, I know we can."

At a call for silence, all movement in the building ceased and they strained to listen for the sound that had alerted the NCO.

It was faint, but distinctive and unmistakable, the sound of a large helicopter, flying a methodical search pattern.

"Not that it's my nature to be a prophet of doom," from the window of the garage office Ripper watched the chopper turning to begin yet another sweep, "but I been taking a long hard look at the major's map, and it kinda seems to me that the pilot of that there whirlybird is hovering plumb over the top of a patch of ground we got to pass through. Don't you think there's a better than fair chance that he is going to do something right unsociable to us?"

"He's going to try." Having checked the Grail as far as he was able without comprehensive test equipment, Libby began to reassemble it, cleaning and making a final check of every component as he did so.

"I knew a girl once . . ."

"Another cousin?"

"Funny you should ask that, 'cause as it happens she was, about four times removed. Anyway, she were right uppity 'bout just about everything. Not a single fella I knew had ever got near her. You know she were going on sixteen and still a virgin. Where I come from, a girl who gets to that age and ain't been treated to a roll in the hay, she's either got to be ugly as sin, sewn up, or a damned fine runner. Like I were saying, nobody had got nowhere, not until her folks got a TV."

"Perhaps to your yokel mentality the connection is obvious," Cline had tried, and failed to work it out for himself, "but do you think you could explain that?"

"Sure. She couldn't read."

"So help me, I'm going to hit him in a minute." Making a special effort, Cline persevered. "What's that got to do with anything?"

"Just about everything. See, she had this problem, not the one your friends won't tell you about, the sort you can't ask your friends about, you with me? Jesus, you guys are thick. She had this itch, now you with me? In a kinda personal place, like underneath. Not being able to read she'd not seen no ads in the papers, didn't even know she could get anything for it until they tuned into a commercial station for the first time. Must have went straight out and bought a case of ointment. Last I heard she was screwing like a rabbit, had ten kids and was trying to catch herself a husband."

"God, they get worse." Cline stepped aside to let Dooley in.

"Shit, have I missed story time?"

"I could tell you the one about my Aunt Martha, who had the accident with the billy goat and the broom handle."

"Save it." Cline backed out. "I can only take so much of this at a time."

"That's what Aunt Martha said."

Dooley took Libby aside. "What was the major saying about refugees?"

"He wasn't. Why, are you thinking to make their misery complete by diddling them out of the little they've got?"

"Alright, don't get touchy, I only asked, no harm in that, is there?"

It took little imagination to figure out what the big American was after. Libby wouldn't be a party to any crooked schemes he might be hatching. Not that all the refugees were lily-white. Among them there were some of the nastiest individuals alive. The bunch Andrea had been with were prime examples. Russian deserters, ex-border guards, criminals, all had formed armed gangs and preyed on the weak and defenceless civilians trapped in the Zone. By stealing food, by brutality, by reducing the people's will to live, they were responsible for as many deaths as the shells and mines and bullets.

"You got that stovepipe working?" Dooley changed the subject. He knew that Libby's knowledge of the refugees was extensive, there was always a chance he could milk him of it piece by piece, provided he stayed on his right side.

"Far as I can tell, yes. Since when have you been interested in anything except making the next buck?"

"Think what you like. I just thought you might like to know I heard Hyde and the major talking things over. Seems you're going to hand the turret over to Clarence, and then sit out the top with that thing, ready to do a spot of chopper hunting." Dooley waited for a reaction—there was none.

Expecting some such arrangement, the news came as no surprise to Libby, would not have bothered him even if he'd been unprepared for it. In a way it was as though he were packing months of combat into a few hours, an unconscious last fling. The girl's words came back to him. He hadn't spoken to her since, and didn't feel he could now.

The rage had passed, a calm filled his mind, totally unlike his usual mental state in battle. It occurred to him that perhaps in some strange way he was being made ready for death, but he couldn't believe that. Not that he was unready for it. When it did come it would be almost welcome, though his last moments would be a torment if Helga's fate was still unknown.

From the workshop came the growl of the APC's engines being restarted. Picking up the launcher, Libby followed Cline back to their transport. The bombardier was putting on his keen and eager act for their officer's benefit. Let him. A week ago it would have annoyed Libby, now he didn't care.

He stood half out of the rear hatch as they backed away from the workshop, having to duck the low doorway. There was no sign of the chopper, and the noise of their own engines drowned any distant sound of it.

They were racing towards the area it had been quartering, making up time, putting in distance. The sun was sinking low in the sky and, only partially filtered by the dust in the air, glowed a bright vision-blurring orange straight into his face. Libby set the missile tube to his shoulder, braced himself against the rough ride and just waited. There was no need for him to strain himself. The gunship would come to them.

THIRTEEN

Coming at them out of the sun, Libby heard the helicopter gunship before he saw it. At two thousand feet it swept overhead, and swivelling round to keep tracking it over the open sights of the launcher, Libby felt the rough metal of the hatch opening cut into his leg.

It made a tight banking turn for a second pass, and he had to pan fast as he applied light pressure to the trigger, activating the missile's own seeker-system. The top mounted warning light turned from red to green as the tracker locked on to the chopper's hot jetpipe, and Libby pulled the trigger back all the way.

The boost charged fired, and burning out almost instantly, propelled the slim grey-painted missile several yards from the mouth of the tube before the solid fuelled sustainer ignited and accelerated the five and a half pound warhead on its way.

It was immediately obvious that the pilot or one of his crew had seen the launch, as the gunship turned even tighter in an attempt to bring itself head-on to the missile, when the infra-red homing device would have the smallest target, only the extreme tip of the jetpipes.

For a moment, as the missile wavered in its arcing course it looked as if the standard tactic would work, and it almost did. Had the warhead not been fitted with a fuse activated by grazing contact, it would have.

Helicopter and missile closed fast, with the aircraft speed far exceeded by the projectile's one and a half times the speed of sound.

Exploding alongside the starboard turboshaft engine, it caused the helicopter to lurch and then roll almost on to its side. Trailing smoke and shedding fragments of metal it began to fall, then partially recovered to commence a staggering descent that was still far too fast.

At five hundred feet the pilot succeeded in regaining a degree of control and the rate of descent slackened and the drunken side-slipping began to diminish. Then a damaged rotor blade snapped off halfway along its length, and before whirling clear sliced the tips from two others.

Violent shudders shook the craft as it stalled, and then it began to drop. The last four hundred feet it plummeted vertically, impacting on the top of a hill. Crushed by the weight of the twin Isotov engines the cabin collapsed, and then its ruin was hidden as fuel ignited and the ammunition started to cook-off.

"How come he didn't let us have it?" From the next hatch Cline had watched the engagement. "He had a full load, rockets and gun pods. The bugger could have smeared us over the landscape at the first pass."

"That is not so difficult to explain." Boris elbowed his way up to see the spectacle for himself from the same hatch. "Someone wants us alive, there can be no other reason."

Libby tossed the launch tube over the side, following its progress down a steep embankment to land among large stones at the edge of a stream. "That gives us an advantage then, if the Ruskies are going to be pulling their punches."

"For a moment, yes." Boris pushed back, resisting the bombardier's attempt to cram him into a corner of the opening. "But it is likely that as we near our own lines the orders will be changed. If whoever wants us cannot have us alive, then he will be happy to settle for us dead."

"Well, it was only a bloody makeshift repair." Burke resented the carping from Dooley and the others, as the APC struggled to climb the hill on one engine. "What sort of job do you think I can fucking do with a couple of spanners, a wrench and some ruddy string?"

As the gradient grew steeper, their progress became slower and slower, until it was obvious that the transport was not going to make it to the brow.

"It's all damned hills from here on in." Revell folded his map and tucked it into his pocket. "There looks to be a track, or a fire-break up ahead. See if we can make it to that, then take us in."

They were only inching forward when Burke turned them on to the conifer-lined, deeply rutted track. Grass had long since hidden the wheel marks but the corrugations remained and the long vehicle rose and fell as though in a swell.

"Hold it." Half-hidden among trees that had grown to envelop it, a noticeboard stood at the side of the track. There was an indecipherable symbol at its top, and his scant German was no help in reading the near illegible words beneath, their lettering also victims of the sun's fading, and the weather-induced flaking of the red paint. "What is it, mines?"

Andrea squeezed forward, and allowed herself a tight smile as she let the tension build a little longer. "There is a penalty if you go beyond this point, but only if you leave litter on the picnic ground."

"Hey, now that ain't funny." Ripper pulled out the flak-jacket he had been sitting on from beneath him. "Next time just come straight out with it. Thinking you might lose your balls is damned near as unpleasant as doing it."

"And what would you do without your nuts?" Hyde laid the sarcasm on thickly.

"I'll tell you, Sarge. Afore I came out here, I asked my doc' what would happen if I lost my little bag of marbles. A fella ought to know about these things, it pays to be prepared."

"So . . . go on."

"Seems if your tool ain't included in the damage, you still got a mite of screwing time left, before your hormones start to get real mixed up, and you end up getting screwed yourself."

With the last ounce of power, Burke parked the APC beneath the canopy provided by a stand of mature pines, as the temperature of their remaining engine finally crossed into the red under the loads that had been imposed on it. When he switched off, the smell of hot oil filled the compartment.

"All change." Ripper's loudly proclaimed reference to their earlier form of transport earned him a growled, spanner-waving threat from their driver, which he ignored.

Burke paid for his display of ill-humour, dropping the rusty tool as he climbed out, and having to scramble on his hands and knees to look for it in the gloom, among the heaped needles of the forest floor.

Taking off his helmet, and resting his rifle against a tree, Ripper breathed deeply and did a few gentle setting-up exercises. "Now this is a better place to break down. Will you get a load of that air."

Even as he had climbed from the APC, the heavy scent of the pines had struck Libby, washing the taints of stale sweat and cordite and oil from his lungs. It was intensely quiet, the trees and springy surface underfoot absorbing every sound without echo. When the engine covers were thrown open the disturbing noise was of short duration, as though the forest had dampened and abbreviated it.

With every step large cones rolled beneath his feet, crunching and crackling as they were crushed into the carpet of slim brown spikes. But that, like the distant call of a wood pigeon, did not disturb the sombre mood of the place.

"Be a nice place to live, up here." Through the stiffly standing trunks Libby could see along the track where it curved down the hillside. The trees lining it framed the sunset, now made a blotchy red by the dust clouds it shone through. Fog was hiding the details of the lowlands, only a few soft-contoured hills standing like islands upon it to give any point of reference.

Bending down to pick up a handful of the deep covering of needles, Dooley let them run out through his fingers as he straightened. "Yeah, you could be right. Ground like this would soak up a lot of slurry."

"Don't you ever think about anything but pig shit?"

Dooley treated the sniper's question seriously. "Of course I do, sometimes, when I'm on a forty-eight hour. But right now we're in the Zone. While we're here, can you think of anything better?"

Using a map board as a tray, Boris was distributing cups of coffee. "This is the last. We have found some soup, enough for a little each, and then there is nothing."

"The nothing sounds better. Someone else can have my share. You found that soup aboard the carrier. No way am I going to eat Russian muck." An incredulous Cline watched Clarence drink at one go the boiling coffee that was burning his fingers even through the thick enamelled mug. "Even if I had a gullet like his I wouldn't, so you know what you can do with your cabbage soup."

"Actually it is *bulyon*, chicken broth, and you would be missing a treat. It is delicious."

"I ain't never had Ruskie food, what's it like?" At the risk of burning his mouth, Dooley was using the unsweetened black coffee like a mouthwash, but swallowing it after swishing it around his gums.

"When you can get it, at its best it is superb, but for

166

a long time now only Party members and senior officers have been able to get enough food of good quality. For most there are only queues, disappointment and growing hunger." Boris thought back to the brief stay he'd spent in Moscow, soon after completing his training. Most, virtually all his time there, had been a hell he'd rather soon forget; but there had been one night, out with a friend who was a well-connected Party member, when he had eaten at a restaurant.

"The best meal I ever had was in Moscow. There the Party fat cats take good care of themselves, and once, just once, I saw what it was like. I started with smoked salmon, do you know I had never even seen it before; and with it a glass of chilled vodka, Stolichnaya, the very best. Then there was chicken breasts filled with butter, so rich, so full that it splashed my best uniform but I did not care. And then I had ice-cream with three kinds of fresh fruit and then brandy with Turkish coffee. When I got back to my barracks I was sick. And then I served ten days in military prison for the damage to my uniform, and I never wanted to eat well again."

"I still prefer German chow . . ."

"Good, then I'll help you work up an appetite for pork and spuds," Hyde interrupted. He indicated a tall tree. "Shin up that and keep a watch for aircraft. We could miss them from down here. Not much we can do about them, but we might as well be prepared for whatever they call down on us."

"Fuck that. I'm not a bloody monkey."

"Do it." There was no inflexion, no irritation in Hyde's voice.

"And if I don't?" Dooley stood his ground, though a fraction less sure of himself. He noticed the others had moved away from him. The sergeant was carrying his rifle.

"You're right, I can't make you. Apart from the fact I wouldn't waste a bullet on you, if I did you'd be in no state to climb. So I tell you what, if you don't fancy doing it, just nip over and tell the major. He's watching you now."

"Anybody got a banana?" Throwing his assault rifle to Ripper, Dooley hitched his trousers and started up the tree.

Ripper watched him go. "Hell, I don't know what the Commie bombers might drop on us, but sure as eggs is eggs, it couldn't be as bad as if he does."

"I fucking heard that, you shitty pox-faxed hill-billy."

"He sure do have a way with words, don't he?" Ripper tried his coffee, and found it had gone cold. "You lousy bastard, listening to you and Boris I've let my coffee go cold, it's all your damned fault. What you gonna do about it?"

From somewhere above them floated Dooley's response. "Oh hell, I am sorry. Tell you what, I'll make it up to you, I'll let you have something warm of mine."

There was a brief pause, and then the trees shivered and sent down a deluge of needles as a long loud fart shook the forest.

When Ripper looked down again, many of them were floating, or in the course of sinking, in his coffee.

*   *   *

The white sickle of the new moon gave just sufficient light to work by as Burke toiled at the broken pump. "Sodding awful this Russian equipment. No wonder they always rely on bloody numbers when they fight. They need to send a hundred of these crates into battle to make sure ten reach our lines."

"And then they find they're facing only two of ours." Libby tested the strength of the drive belt he had improvised from various pieces of webbing, putting his foot in it like a stirrup and pulling as hard as he could. "Be nice for us to surprise the Commies for once. Even this blooming Kothen show was a shambles. Some light flak . . . I'd like to meet the staff officer who wrote that."

Cline sat by them. He shifted uneasily, alternately cradling his Russian rifle, and nervously pointing it towards the heart of the forest. "You hear anything?"

He got only negatives from the men busy with the engine, and craned forward, turning an ear towards the direction of the sound he thought he had heard. "You sure you don't hear anything?"

"Either shut up, or go for a trot and check it out." The would-be belting had snapped, and Libby's temper was also close to doing so.

"I'll just have a look around then." He held back a moment, but no one urged him to stay put, and he began to shuffle cautiously towards the darkness beneath the trees further in.

Shit, this was when war got stupid. If he got killed now, with no one looking, who'd ever care? Not this lot, that was for sure. It was alright charging into a dangerous situation when there were officers around to be impressed and write out recommendations for medals, but dying for nothing, that was just plain pathetic.

It was eerie beneath the trees and near pitch-black. There were noises, he could hear them, but it was probably only animals and he wasn't going to make a prat of himself over a false alarm. Perhaps it was wolves, didn't they have them in Germany, or maybe escaped animals from an abandoned safari park?

A twig snapped behind him, and he stiffened. Was that a footfall? He had a round chambered, and was tempted to fire, just to break the predominating silence. He could always explain it away as an accident. But this lot of cruds would see through that.

Remembering the image intensifier Revell had lent him, he groped for it on his chest, where it hung from the cord about his neck. As he lifted it there was another sound behind him, and he had no time to react as a noose was dropped over his head and jerked tight.

Libby heard the strangled shout that abruptly died in a choking splutter, and was reaching for his rifle and calling the alarm before the webbing he dropped had touched the ground.

A dark shape came at him from behind a tree and he blocked the knife thrust at him with his rifle butt. Another figure came at him from the side and he went down beneath it as he was knocked off balance.

Two short jabbing blows he connected elicited a soft groan from his assailant, who collapsed and lay still. There were fights all around him; the others were being attacked as they jumped from the APC.

With sweeping blows Dooley hurled three attackers from him, and was about to deliver a stamp of his boot on the face of the nearest, when by the flash of a single shot close by he saw it was a young girl.

Others of the squad had seen similar things, and the fighting stopped abruptly. Cline staggered from the trees, retching loudly and trying with his free hand to ease the knot that bound his other, still holding the imaging device tight into his throat. "What the fuck is going on? I've just had to clobber an old lady. She was trying to kill me."

Several of the women were out cold or semi-conscious and had to be dragged to join the others herded together by the APC. An assortment of knives and improvised clubs had been taken from them.

"You want me to search them?" Dooley stepped forward, volunteering for the first time ever.

Revell motioned Andrea to do it, and she worked through them briskly and thoroughly, her frisking producing another two knives, a meat cleaver and a hatchet.

"Not very ladylike are they?" Hyde toed the collection. His back stung where a length of wood had been swung into it by a girl who now nursed a broken wrist, and was crying gently.

There was confusion among the women as they heard English being spoken, a dark-haired middle-aged member of the group took a step forward. "You are British?"

"And American, yes."

At the answer the woman fell to her knees, clasped Revell around the thighs and, resting her head against him, burst into tears. He tried to push her away, but couldn't break his hold without using greater force than he wanted to, but she sensed his displeasure and let go.

It took three attempts before she regained control of herself and stood up, wiping her dirt-streaked face with a startlingly white handkerchief. "I'm sorry. It is just that we have been through so much. And now we are safe . . ."

She looked about, and the relief in her face changed to doubt as she took in the unmistakable outline of the Russian vehicle. "There are others? You have come to push the Russians back, yes? We saw your helicopters fly over, and heard the fighting. We are safe now, aren't we?"

There was no way to soften the blow, and Revell watched her face crumple into tears again as he told her the true position. This time they were not tears of joy, and flowed faster.

With Andrea's help Libby had been checking the women's injuries. "Not too bad, Major. A few cracked ribs, a broken wrist and one bullet wound, a nice clean hole through an arm, hardly bleeding. The rest is just cuts and bruises, and we've got nearly as many of those. They fought like damned tigers."

"Do what you can to fix them up. I'll try and sort out what the hell is going on."

"Want to swop jobs?"

The offer was made by Dooley, as Libby helped a girl out of her jacket and she whimpered with the pain of her fractured hand. "Piss off. Most of this lot are too young for your warped tastes."

"What do you reckon they are, a mobile knocking shop, sort of stop-me-and-fuck-one?" Dooley found the idea attractive, and kept trying to catch the eye of one woman, but she avoided his stare.

"Leave off. Not every damned woman in the Zone chucks herself on her back at every opportunity. Some of these are only kids. All they're trying to do is reach the West. Think of the state they must have been in to take the risk."

"Alright Sir Galahad, point taken, keep your shirt on." He couldn't resist it, Dooley made a last attempt to get some recognition from the woman, then failing again, and being shoved aside by Libby, he moved off.

Having calmed her, Revell had sat the dark-haired woman on a fallen tree and joined her. "Why did you attack us? It was a hell of a risk to take, without much chance of success."

"We were desperate. Some of our people are hurt, and we could not go on. When we saw you arrive we knew you would have something we need, and we had to take the risk, it was our only hope. I do not know the word for it, I will show you. Will you come with me?"

His hesitation was only momentary, then Revell accepted her hand and let her lead him into the trees. They did not go far. She stopped before a great pile of heaped pine branches and began to pull them away.

Revell stepped forward to help, and as he lifted the first armful, heard the distinctive click of a pistol being cocked.

FOURTEEN

"Nein, nein, American!"

As the woman hissed the urgent announcement the last branches fell away and Revell found himself looking into the open back of a long-wheelbase Land-Rover.

Two heavily bandaged men were laid on the side benches. One was deeply unconscious with blood seeping from the dressings of a head wound. The other, both legs splinted and his bare chest bound with windings of what looked like torn shirts and blouses, held a pistol and was unsteadily waving it in Revell's direction.

The woman climbed in and gently took it from his hand. As though the effort had been too much, the man fell back and his eyes closed as his breath wheezed in and out from a blood-flecked mouth.

"They tried to steal from a Russian camp, and were seen. We managed to get them back here, but unless we can repair our transport they cannot go further. If we stay we will die, if we go on we will kill them. And we are not strong, our food ran out two days ago and I do not think we could carry them far."

"By the look of them you wouldn't need to." There was a distinctive smell coming from both men, the slightly sickly-sweet smell of the early stage of putrefaction, soon it would turn to a stomach churning stench as gangrene took a hold and an already certain death would come sooner and be more painful for them, and more distressing for those with them.

"You could leave them."

She shook her head. "They are my brother and his son. I could not do that. And now the others look to me as their leader, and would not go on without me, so . . ." She left the sentence hanging.

"Let me see what the trouble is with this wagon. They're pretty tough, not much will put them out of action."

Getting out, and moving round the side of the vehicle, the woman uncovered a large square object on the ground. "As I said, we managed to pick them up after the attempt to get food failed, but a Russian sentry did this. We got away, but after we stopped to attend to Helmut and Joseph could not get started again. It was then we discovered the damage."

There was a hole in the battery. Made by a high-velocity bullet it had passed through without doing much more than starring the casing about the neat entry and exit points, even the plates appeared to have escaped damage, but all of the fluid had drained away save for a half-inch in the bottom.

Revell used matches to check over the rest of the Land-Rover, and discovered no other hits. The only bullet hole had been made by that which had gone on to immobilize the vehicle. "I think there's a chance we can fix this for you, get you on your way again."

"You will take us with you? You must. It has taken us a week to get this far, travelling only by night. It could take as long again to finish the journey, and that will be too long."

"I'm sorry, that's not possible. The Russians are looking for us, and we would only draw attention to you. Wait until a few hours after we leave, we will have drawn them off by then, and you should make good time. That's the best I can offer. You must tell the others that, and then I will give you some dressings and send you back with my driver. He should be able to fix the battery. We can give you a tow to start, before we pull out."

As they walked back to the APC she said nothing. It was as though she had been drained of emotion. She had known every one in the last few days and each more painful, more intense than the previous, they had leeched much of the spirit that had brought her and the others this far.

"Sergeant Hyde." On their return Revell immediately noticed that the NCO had given the men tasks that would keep them away from the women. Except for Libby, who worked closely with Andrea, tending the injured. He hated seeing that, someone else close to her, when he couldn't be. Damn her, his bitch of an ex-wife had always been able to sparkle when they were with others, and then had drooped or gone cold when they were alone together, usually at bedtime.

"Major?" Hyde could see where the officer was looking, and knew why. What the hell, he wasn't going to arrange things especially to make an officer's love life easier, or his frustration less.

"Eh, yes." Damn he must be getting tired, his attention had wandered, but then it often did towards Andrea. It was a good job none of the others noticed. "We've no way of knowing how that shot carried. Sound plays tricks at night. Put a watch on the track, just in case. Put Dooley on it first. He was only up the tree a short time before it got dark, and it'd be as well to get him away from the women."

Crud, shitty crud. Fucking shitty crud. The shitty bastard. Dooley knew the order originated from the major. Shit. What harm would it have done for him to have stayed back there, trying to chat up the women? With everyone looking he'd have hardly been likely to have got anywhere, but it made a nice change, or would have, to have a bit of feminine company. He didn't count Andrea. Apart from the fact she went off on her own and squatted when she had a pee, she was just the same as one of the men.

Three months she had hung around him, pumping him for knowledge, learning all there was to know about close-quarters fighting, even getting him to give her Kung-Fu lessons, and what had he got for it? A couple of crafty squeezes at a very nice firm tit, his face up against her arse a couple of other times and one lovely and all too brief grind on top of her before she'd realized what he was doing. He could still feel that hard contact with the tight-closed top of her legs, and then the beautiful slide forward to run his erection up her denim-covered crack. And he could still feel the pain as she had ripped out a handful of his hair in hurling him off, and the kick to his balls with which she had finished that lesson, and nearly his sex-life for good.

The last three weeks, though, she'd hardly come to him at all, she'd learnt all she could and pretty soon she'd be fastening on to someone else. Maybe it'd be Libby, he'd already noticed them together a couple of times, but somehow he didn't think so. Whatever the reason though, it was getting up Revell's nose, and in that at least Dooley could find some measure of revenge for the stinking, lousy, crappy numbers the major was pulling at the moment.

Clarence arrived to take over, and very stiffly Dooley vacated the warm soft depression he'd made in the grass. As he'd expected, the sniper chose his own spot and he watched him settle down, after first carefully laying out a groundsheet.

Taking a last look at the track, standing in the pale moonlight like a broad silver stream between the canyon walls of the trees, Dooley started back to the APC. He was tired, but had gone beyond the stage where he could sleep. If they made it back he'd sleep then, probably round the clock, and if they didn't then he wouldn't need it.

"Can I talk to you?"

Coming out of the darkness, without warning, the voice made him jump. A woman stepped in front of him. The one whose eye he had been trying to catch.

"Please, can I talk to you?" She held her hands tight-clasped in front of her, crushing a silk scarf between them.

"Yeah, I suppose so." He was wary, in case it was

a trap.

"I have three children with me, my daughters."

Now Dooley was really on his guard. It sounded almost like an offer, but it couldn't be. He said nothing, waiting to see what came next.

"They are very pretty; very pretty." There was a catch in her voice. "I am afraid of what will happen if those Russian animals find them."

She had leant against him, and he could feel the gentle warmth of her full body. "You'll have to talk to the major, I can't help you, I'm not in charge."

"Please, he will not listen to me. I have tried, but he says there will be greater danger if we go with you."

"He's right." Dooley put his arms around her and held her to him, comforting her by stroking her hair. "Someone in the Ruskie high command has got it in for us. Wherever we go, all hell breaks loose."

"It is not for me. All I have left is my girls. My husband was killed by the Communists when he stopped them from raping our youngest. Greta was only fifteen at the time. They are my life. I have kept them safe, and now I want only for them to reach the West and learn of freedom; freedom from fear and from want. You like me, I know you do. You must help me."

No one, absolutely no one had ever got through to him like this before. He felt his eyes growing hot and moist as he hugged her close. In her he felt softness, warmth and compassion; all the things he had ever looked for in a woman. And there was nothing he could do, nothing.

"Your officer says that we must follow some hours behind. Is there nothing else we can do?"

When she looked up at him it seemed the most natural thing in the world to do. He kissed her, a kiss that started as a token and finished long afterwards as a passionate joining of two people who had found something they needed.

"You don't have to wait 'til we're over the hill." The embrace had taken his breath away and Dooley had to break and pause before he could speak. "He's not going to shoot you off the road, Christ, we're not shitty Commies. Soon as you get started, hang in behind us and we'll lead you through, what can he do?"

This time her mouth sought his, and as they met her tongue forced contact with his. Dooley's hand closed over her large soft breast and felt for the contours of her body beneath the layers of clothing.

As he fumbled with the fastenings of her clothing he caught the faint whiff of perfume and the thought occurred that perhaps she had engineered this, but he didn't care. His penis was iron hard, she was ready for him and he wanted her.

He hated clothes, the delay and clumsy fumblings they brought to something that should be so natural and spontaneous, but with her hands reaching for his zip and her tongue snaking into his ear the ritual of disrobing was almost a part of pleasure.

The cold night air was suddenly on the lower half of his body and at the same moment he found the waistband of her knickers and began to ease them down over the wide swell of her hips.

Her momentary resistance was also a part of the ritual, and then the tip of his penis was pushing against the soft-backed bush of hair between her legs and he felt a moment's cool dampness before he began to slide into her. He penetrated a little, then felt a barring roughness.

"Not here. Please, let me lie down." Pulling her impaled body from him she waited for his next move.

Dooley had been through this before. Taking off his jacket he laid it on the ground, took her by the hands and gently lowered her on to it. Experience told him there was no point in trying to re-enter immediately, and with the cold creeping into the lower half of his body, and reducing his massive erection to a flaccid shadow of its former self, he worked again through the process of kissing and touching.

She responded, for whatever reason he didn't care, she responded and her fingers closed about his wet-tipped penis and jerked on it to work it to new hardness.

Threading through her many layers of clothing his hand found a nipple, and rolling and teasing it between his fingers he brought it erect, then moving from her lips sought it with his mouth and began to suck and lick at it.

He had to free a hand from behind her to seek her mouth and lay a warning finger across her lips as she involuntarily gave vent to loud moans and gasps.

For an instant he thought she was pushing him away, then realized she was trying to engineer a change of position. He eased back from her and she turned half on to her stomach so that his erection was prodding the twin crescents of her backside. An exploratory prod was met by muscle-clenching resistance.

Not sure what she wanted, he let his hand roam over her buttock and thigh and around to her front where it slid through the luxuriant tangle of her pubic hair and into her moist opening.

Now she responded with force, ramming her bottom back into his lap, and pulling upwards so that his tip ran down the tight groove of her bottom to the deep indent at the top of her legs. And then he knew what she wanted. While with practised touch he worked on her with his fingers from the front, his penis sought her body from behind and when it found it entered with well-lubricated ease.

It was the best he had ever had. Her hand guided his, pressing him to the soft yielding places between her tight-clenched thighs while he strove to make every second count as he thrust and withdrew and thrust again to use every available inch of her body.

When he came he lost control, pumping first deep inside her, then pulling out and feeling the release as he finished on the backs of her legs.

Expecting her to make a fuss, complain at what he had done, as he pulled away he sought for a piece of rag or handkerchief to offer. But she didn't, turning on her back and pulling up her underclothes and then smoothing down her skirt.

"You were good. You made no demands."

It was the first time a woman had ever said that to him, Dooley didn't know quite how to take it. In part it was certainly a compliment, but the rest? To hell with it. He'd had a good one, a fucking good one, and so had she, she'd said so, as good as.

And now reaction set in. There was no strength left in him. It would have been good to lay with her, exploring her body with hands and tongue while she did the same for him, until they were ready to do it again, but he was too tired.

"Now it is my turn."

He didn't believe what he'd heard. "You've got to be joking. You've just sucked the life out of me."

"And it was good for you, I was pleased you did it the way I wanted, but this time you do it just for me. It does not matter whether you come or not." She put her hand up her skirt and did something to herself. "Some of what you did is on my clothes, if I scream who would your officer believe?"

"You cow. Just don't blame me if I'm no good."

"Oh, I will help you." Going down on her knees she unfastened Dooley. "See, already it is almost possible, just a little more . . ."

Her hands were at him, rubbing, kneading, pulling. It occurred to him that this is what it must be like for a woman, being used. He couldn't help himself, he was going hard.

"Good, now you are ready. Oh, come on, join in, you will enjoy it." Backing him against a tree she ground against his body, hoisting her skirt to feel the tip of his penis against her wet underwear.

She wasn't pulling them down, just aside, and as she guided him in the lace-trimmed hem cut into the base of his erection. His shoulders ached as she gripped him, pulling herself up and down, going faster and faster as she strove for her climax. As it reached a stage where he really thought he could take no more she changed to short deliberate strokes and the intolerable roughness of the action was replaced by flooding damp as she achieved her orgasm.

It took an age, as she drew out the sensation, almost pulling off him then sliding down once more and gasping and groaning as other spasms of pleasure coursed through her.

Finishing at last, she pulled away, straightened her clothes, and without another word or sign walked off to rejoin the others.

Dooley tucked himself back in, finding the stickiness left by her body distasteful, rubbing himself on his clothing to remove it.

He'd done it so many times himself, and now something like it had happened to him, and he didn't like it. But at least the woman had let him come. A lot of times with his women he'd only satisfied himself, taking no account of their needs, not even considering them, not even thinking of them. Under other circumstances he would have strolled back, getting ready to boast of yet another conquest, but this time he didn't feel he could . . . didn't want to.

What had happened was not of his doing. He had just been an instrument, an animated vibrator and he did not enjoy thinking of himself in that way.

So what the hell, he'd just forget it, push it to the back of his mind. But when he bent to pick up his rifle the cold damp tackiness in his pants and the aching soreness told him it would not be that easy.

Shit, the fucking woman had turned his world upside down, he would never be just the hunter again. In future it would always be in his mind that he might be the prey, and even when he could be sure of the relative relationships, when he had a woman over whom he had total domination, then what it was like for her would still be creeping into the back of his mind, and he would not be doing it just for himself.

He sat with his back to a tree in sight of their transport. It was possible to make out the huddled forms of the women, most of whom had stayed here, rather than going back to their Land-Rover.

Perhaps they didn't trust Revell, or more likely they were just scared. It would have taken a lot of courage in the first place to put the abandoned vehicle back into working order and provision it for their escape to the West. That would have taken weeks, months, perhaps a year or more, while they tried to acquire spare parts without raising suspicion and, putting a little of their meagre ration aside each week, accumulated a supply that might last them the journey.

To anyone who had not been in the Zone it was impossible to visualize the difficulties of travel within it, especially for those without permission to do so.

The refugees were ruled with an iron rod by the Russians, had to stay put, fend as best they could within the prescribed area about their camp. For the Communists the civilians were simply another form of camouflage, to be moved and rearranged as the need arose.

And for those who did make the break, who tried to reach the West, simply evading the Russian patrols was just the start. Minefields, ground surveillance radar linked to machine guns firing on fixed lines; areas where persistent toxic chemicals still lingered and territory heavily irradiated by atomic air bursts, all those had to be avoided, with movement limited to the hours of darkness. The wonder was not that some made it to the West, but that any ever tried.

The group they had met up with, they would have been through all that already, and now after days of hunger and constant fear they were near the limit of their endurance. Their abortive attack on what they'd thought to be a Russian patrol had been their last fling.

What would his last fling be? Dooley had never given it a thought before. Maybe he'd just had it. When the repairs were completed they would be off again, driving fast towards whatever nastiness the Russians had in store for them next.

His eyes felt heavy, and his head dropped forward on to his chest. He knew he was falling asleep, could feel it stealing up on him, and didn't resist. Letting his mind drift it came back time and time again to the recent experience with the woman. She had used him . . . that worried him . . . he didn't want that to be his last fling . . .

"Fat stiff." Burke had seen Dooley follow the woman from the trees, and now as he reassembled the water pump saw him nodding off. He felt like throwing something. "How come everything always goes his way? Look at him, he doesn't have a bloody care in the world. Christ, you wouldn't think he was in the ruddy Zone would you?"

"I expect he has problems, worries." At last Libby was satisfied with the strength of the belting he had made.

"Him, never. Eating, fucking and fighting, that's all he thinks about. His only problem is getting enough of them. He's forgotten that woman already."

"Maybe not." Libby gave the belt a final test, and it passed. "Maybe not."

HEADQUARTERS. AIR DEFENCE COMMAND. CENTRAL SECTOR. ZONE.

The telephone kept slipping in General Pakovski's moist grip. He could feel sweat trickling down inside his uniform, soaking the back of his jacket. "... Yes, Comrade Lieutenant General, they are the only ones who have broken out ... Yes, every effort ... I understand Comrade Lieutenant General, you have given Moscow assurances on the strength of those I gave you ... Three more hours, thank you, Comrade Lieutenant General ..."

Before he finished speaking, Pakovski heard the line go dead, but he completed the sentence for the sake of appearance; the colonel was in the room. "Where are they now?"

On the wall map the colonel circled a patch of forest on the western border of the Harz nature park. "They are here, Comrade General. The local commander says the ground is too difficult for armour, but he has managed to move two battalions of light infantry into the area, and they are attempting an encirclement. He says it will be difficult to take them alive if they should fight ..."

"They are getting too close to their own lines, now I want them dead." Pakovski could tell there was something else. His snap made it no easier for the colonel to broach the subject. "Well, what is it?"

189

"Eh, it is just that the infantry commander has questioned the authority of your orders, as have the air units you have ordered to join the search . . ."

"Say what ever you have to, threaten, promise, bribe: I must have the group destroyed. That is all that matters. I will deal with the other problems afterwards."

As the colonel went out, the general took his pistol from its polished holster and laid it on the desk in front of him. He had intended to use it on the survivors of the NATO group. Now, unless they could be wiped out, it would have to serve another purpose.

FIFTEEN

They were about to give the Land-Rover a tow start behind the APC when the first star shell ignited with a loud "crack" several thousand feet above the tree tops.

Night was washed from the forest by the harsh glare and replaced by searing white light in which the boundaries of shadows were marked with knife-edged precision.

"Russian infantry, bloody thousands of them. All around us." Cline was out of breath, and the fast passage he had made down the hillside to be sure of being the first to report had marked his face and hands with long livid cuts from whipping spike-tipped branches.

Standing half-out of a roof hatch, Revell sensed rather than saw the quality of the light diminish as the flare sank lower, and looked up in time to see it replaced by another high overhead. "How long before they reach us?"

"Five minutes. They're just coming on like a load

of zombies."

"OK, pull the sentries back. We'll have to try and crash out of here."

As Hyde bent down to detach the wire hawser from the Land-Rover's two-tiered front bumper he was pushed away by the dark-haired women.

"You must take us with you."

"There's no armour on your transport, you'll be a big soft target for everything that misses us." In her voice Revell could hear a blend of begging and demanding and pleading. "You don't know the risks."

"We do, but more than that we know what will happen if we stay, when those animals find us. Please, you must take us, we accept the risk: you cannot leave us for them."

A star shell, its fiery magnesium filling not totally consumed, fell through the trees thirty yards away and as its parachute snagged, started a blaze among tinder-dry lower branches. White smoke began to wreathe the base of the trees about it, held down by the interwoven canopy above.

With the air filling with the sweet, biting scent of hot pine resin, Revell saw a chance. He tossed the vehicle's signal pistol to the sergeant. "See what you can do to stoke that, but try not to fry us."

Variously coloured balls of blinding fire bounced through the trees, and where they lodged became the seat of secondary blazes that began to merge into a single wall of smoke-shrouded flame.

Burke started forward cautiously, to put the minimum strain on the tow line, and even so felt the snatch as the weight of the Land-Rover was taken up.

With the star shell at their backs, it was the Russian infantry's long shadows he saw first, and then as he rounded the turn in the track they were only twenty yards in front. A snap-fired rocket toppled a tree alongside and as other launchers were levelled he threw the APC through a tight turn and drove it straight at the wood-fed inferno.

The roar of the flames blotted out the noise of the engines, the sound of trees going down before the armoured vehicle's raked front. Smoke filled the interior and fire licked at vision blocks and weapon ports.

Emerging from that hell of their own creation, they immediately ran into straggling lines of enemy infantry that had been halted by the burning trees. Several were mown down, caught by the wide hull or crushed by evergreens snapped off by its pounding progress.

Every round for the heavy machine gun expended, Libby traversed the turret and used an AK74 from a vision port to give what cover he could to the Land-Rover.

Bucking and leaping over every obstacle, he could see the woman at the wheel wrestling to keep the sturdy vehicle in the APC's wake. A body flopped about in the seat beside her, restored to life by every jolt and with each movement spattering the inside of the starred windscreen with pink-tinged brain matter from its bullet-smashed forehead.

Showers of anti-tank rockets flew past. Some impacted against the trunks of trees almost at the moment of launch and broke up to throw back in their operator's face the blazing contents of their propellant section. The forest was made still more hellish by the staggering fiery apparitions those accidents created.

Other rounds ricocheted from tree to tree, until they self-destructed over some group of infantry, or found a mark among them.

A hand grenade detonated between the APC and its tow, and the Land-Rover came through the fireball stained with bars of soot and covered in forest litter. Tracer that failed to penetrate the eight-wheeler's well-angled thick hull plates met no such resistance from the thin vertical walls of the Land-Rover's hardtop.

Twice, Libby saw tracer whose source he could not engage plunge in through the drab painted aluminum; the second time a long burst that stitched a close-spaced row of neat holes the length of its side.

And then they were through, fresh clean air began to replace the choking cordite-tainted smoke and the chemically coloured fires and lines of tracer were being left behind. But there was one more obstacle.

Parked across the junction of track and road was a long nose-to-tail line of Soviet-made trucks. To either side of the track was a drop that in the dark Burke couldn't be sure of negotiating, even without the women's transport in tow. There was only one course open to him.

Drivers leapt from the cabs as the APC charged down on them. At forty miles an hour, the ten-ton machine ploughed into the line, tossing one truck into the air and turning it over, crushing the front of another and having its already damaged spill-board ripped away as it caught in the distorted metal of a vehicle it began to drag with it.

As the metal sheared and the truck was left rocking on its springs the Land-Rover just clipped it, but at that speed the violence of the impact was sufficient to burst open its flimsy rear doors and throw one of the young girls into the road.

Libby saw her tumble and come to rest beside the damaged truck, then reach for the torn metal to pull herself to her feet, one arm hanging limp at her side. He recognised the splint-reinforced bandage about her wrist, and then saw the squat Russian coming around the back of the truck towards her.

Taking very careful aim, Libby loosed off the whole magazine, and saw almost every single round reach its target. Thrown back against the flattened cab, the girl jerked spastically, made her slim body into a high arch, then collapsed and lay still.

He didn't replace the magazine. Instead he un-clipped the three spares from the turret wall and let them drop to the floor of the crew compartment, where Andrea swooped on them, before reluctantly having to part with two.

His hands were shaking, and the effect seemed to be spreading to his whole body. He felt sick, but not in a way that could be explained by his hunger or exhaustion. It was in his mind, and it was as if his brain was whirling around inside his skull. This had to be rock bottom, it couldn't get worse than this, it just couldn't.

The interior of the Land-Rover was like a charnel-house. Both of the men had been hit again, and six of the females had been wounded. Three of them were dying.

Libby knew he was crying, knew that racking sobs were shuddering through his body, but somehow it was as though it was happening to someone else. He felt strangely detached. Even when Sergeant Hyde took him by the shoulders and steered him away from the scene to sit on the parapet of the old stone bridge close by, he felt as if it was another person who was submitting to the hands, taking the steps, sitting on the moss-cushioned hardness of the stone.

A never-ending line of bodies was being formed from the constant stream being carried from the back of the Land-Rover. Through eyes that weren't his own, Libby watched the last dying struggles of the wounded and Dooley covering their faces when all movement finally ceased. First it was the two men, and then one of the women.

Red light filtering weakly from the early dawn picked out and matched the predominating colour of the roadside scene. Everything was red. It stained clothing and hands, covered the road and grass verge and dripped from the vehicle and the injured it had disgorged.

Dooley moved forward to cover another face and as he did was hosed with blood from a rupturing artery deep within a spasm-racked limb. He waited a moment while the fountain subsided to a sluggish welling, then ceased altogether, before drawing the scrap of grubby cloth across the fragment-shattered face.

"Don't drink it." Clarence held a helmet brimful of water in front of Libby. "No way of knowing where it's come from, might have some chemical muck in it."

Libby heard the words, but they weren't for him. They were for the poor devil sitting slumped on the bridge. The face was familiar, but he didn't know anybody who had been through so much that they could look like that. Sunken dark-ringed eyes, made pink and puffy by crying, smoke-stained face barred by streaks of uncontrolled tears. No, he didn't know that person, but he could feel pity for him.

"Splash your face with it. You'll feel better." Clarence felt the helmet being taken from his hands, he looked, and it was Andrea, who dipping in a cloth that tinged the water pink, began to sponge the grime from Libby's hands before rinsing the cloth and starting on his face.

It felt good, cold and clean and fresh. For a moment Libby shared the pleasure of the sensation with the hunched figure, then as the cloth moved over his face it was as though it wiped the confusion from his mind and he knew he was that pitiful creature. As the realisation hit him, so did all the pressures and fears and memories and frustrations that had brought him to that state and his head bowed slowly forward to rest between Andrea's breasts and he cried again.

"Get him aboard." Hyde took Libby's left arm. "We've got to keep moving."

Clarence couldn't do it, took a step back, recoiling from the prospect of physical contact, and it was Andrea who started to take his other arm, before Dooley gently moved her aside and took her place.

Having plugged the several leaks in the Land-

Rover's radiator, and refilled its cooling system from the stream, Burke had at last managed to get the vehicle moving under its own power, though it now produced loud metallic noises from an extravagantly buckled front wheel.

Only three of the wounded women had to be put back on board. When at last they pulled back on to the road, with the Land-Rover trailing the APC by a good quarter of a mile, they left five bodies behind, laid in a neat row beside the road, their open wounds still steaming in the cool morning air.

The area of the Zone through which they were now passing had been fought over quite recently, within the last three months. Wrecked guns and tanks and other vehicles were everywhere.

Carpet bombing, saturation chemical attacks, super-napalm drops, all had contributed towards the utter sterilisation of the landscape. Hardly a plant grew, and the few trees that survived were gouged and splintered by the bombs and shells that had embedded thousands of metal fragments in their bark. The transformation had been so violent it was virtually impossible to tell where the countryside had ended and town had begun. Now the two merged into one, an endless series of crater-scarred low hills.

At the side of the road sat hundreds of burned-out trucks and cars of every description, most of military origin. They lay rusting where the engineers had dumped them, some showing the marks of the heavy bulldozer blades that had shoved them aside when route clearance had become more urgent than salvage.

"Off the road." Even the slamming of the heavy hatch behind him failed to drown out Dooley's shout as he ducked inside.

Burke didn't hesitate, wrenching the steering over and sending the APC into a lightly cratered field that was criss-crossed with the gouge marks of hundreds of sets of tank tracks.

Even as the back wheels hit the mud-surfaced loam, the road behind them erupted in pounding flame as a salvo of air to ground rockets ploughed into it.

"Get us air cover." Revell had to bellow at the top of his voice to be heard by Cline, as the Soviet helicopter gunship banked and rippled another twenty rockets at them.

Fragments rattled and banged against the armour as the close spaced shock waves threatened to push the speeding vehicle over. Having overshot, the chopper had to go into a wide stalling turn to bring it back on target again, and this time Burke was able to watch its head-on approach.

At the first spurt of flame from the launch pods on the gunship's stub wings, their driver put them into a turn that for a moment threatened disaster as they side-swiped a wrecked Abram tank. As the grating sound of the long scraping contact died, he sent them the other way and into the mass of smoke and slowly settling debris from the near misses.

"Hell, don't be stopping now." Ripper looked around at the others, expecting the same reaction

199

from them as their driver slammed on the brakes and slewed the vehicle to a sharp stop then turned off the engine.

Pushing his head up into the turret, Revell slowly cranked it round to take a look at their situation. Their driver had achieved the near impossible, found them a place of concealment in that featureless terrain.

Under cover of the smoke, Burke had parked them between a pair of damaged armoured personnel carriers: on one side a West German Marder, on the other an M113 with Canadian markings. The little group of which they formed the, hopefully, anonymous centrepiece was among a concentration of twenty or more other similar wrecks.

"Shit, what do we do now. Wait for them to fry us?" Shifting position, Ripper tried to move nearer an escape hatch.

"If they do, it will not be yet." With nothing to do while Cline distrustfully worked the radio single-handed, Boris alone found time for the young American. "The gunship will for the moment have lost us among the battlefield litter. If it is a recent model, one of those that has been pared of sophisticated equipment in order that the Communists might indulge their love of numbers above all else, then there is a chance it may not find us before it is forced to break off."

"We'll know soon." Stopped further back, and driven in among the gutted remains of a convoy, Revell was relieved to see that the Land-Rover seemed to have entirely escaped the notice of the gunship, which was continuing to beat back and forth above them. He turned his full attention back to it, in time to see it launch one of its four wire-guided anti-tank missiles.

By the flare at the base of its tail, Revell was able to track the fat-bodied rocket and saw its devastating detonation against the hulk of a burned-out Luch eight-wheeled armoured car. Already leeched by earlier fires of everything combustible, there was no chance that the strike would satisfy the chopper's weapons officer. Without spotting a fire he would know he had not hit his target.

Twice more it circled, and at the end of each turn made a pass over the battlefield and sent down another missile; but lacking the ability to distinguish the live target from the wrecks, only succeeded in further demolishing a pair of already unsalvagable armoured ambulances.

"He'll get tired of pissing about and bugger off in a minute." Lounging back in his seat, Burke jumped violently as a cannon shell exploded against the roof above his head.

In frustration the helicopter crew opened a near continuous fire with their gatling-type fixed armament. The chin-turret mounted weapon sent torrents of shells towards the ground; between bursts they released the last of the 57mm unguided rockets, most of which did no more than turn over ground that had already been churned to a fine tilth by explosives.

"The bastard is trying to flush us out." Dooley made a great show of nonchalantly cleaning his nails with the tip of his bayonet, but spoiled the effect when even he jumped as another round disintegrated on the turret top, and sliced into the tip of a finger. "If that fucker runs out of gas and has to land, I'll fucking have him." He squeezed the base of the finger until its tip went pink then red, and a large bead of dark blood rose from the deep cut.

They listened as the helicopter circled once more, growing fainter as it did so, then at the moment the beat of its motors was on the threshold of their hearing, it began to grow louder, and louder.

"I think he's having one last go." Revell watched its head-on approach, saw its last anti-tank missile spurt from its rail, underslung from the end pylon on the starboard stub wing, saw the light glint briefly on the wires unreeling behind it.

This time he couldn't see the tail flare, only the dark outline of the rocket against the shimmer of its exhaust heat. It took him an instant to realize why the view was so different from those before. He was seeing the warhead not as it homed in on some other target, but as it came at them.

There was no other action he could take. Shouting a warning he dropped to the floor of the compartment and huddled close to it, tucking his head into the crook of his arm.

A giant hammerblow shook the eight-wheeler as the M113 alongside took the full force of a direct hit by the powerful warhead and was moved bodily sideways to crash into the APC. The fireball enveloped all three vehicles and their every external fitting was ripped off by the massive blast.

Feeling the sudden roasting heat on his back,

Revell looked up. All trace of the turret had gone. It had been plucked out neatly, leaving just the ball race and part of the traverse mechanism.

White-hot shafts of molten explosive and metal had sought out every corner of the M113, and discovered a still intact fuel tank. Raised instantly to its flashpoint as it gushed from the leaking container, the fuel now fed a roaring furnace that licked over the squad's partially roofless transport.

Using the top hatches was out of the question, a moment's exposure to the flames would have incinerated them, and the side doors opened only a fraction before making contact with the wrecks between which they were parked.

Flickering tongues of red and yellow played past Burke's vision port as he crunched the APC into gear to drive it out from the clutches of the trap. He pushed the power higher and higher as the machine strained to escape the vice-like hold of the wrecks between which it was now so tightly held. He tried reverse, and the hope the few inches of movement brought was immediately dashed as the vehicle locked solid once again.

The air was becoming unbreathable, and the luxury interior fittings that until now had added a welcome touch of comfort to the usually spartan interior, became an added danger as their varnished finish or foam filling began to heat up, and give off strong fumes.

Packs stowed against the wall licked by the adjoining fires began to smoulder and had to be tossed out through the open roof, some of them to add their content to the fires.

Sergeant Hyde could feel his throat closing, could feel it being constricted by the rasping bite of the poison-filled, oxygen-leeched air. He'd been through this once before and had escaped the flames, though at the terrible cost his deep-burned face revealed: but having cheated the fires once, he wasn't about to let them get him now.

Drawing the pins from the two grenades he'd saved, he reached up until the skin of his hands was being peeled by the fire flaring over the roof, then dropped the steel-wrapped explosive down the carrier's side.

"Forward, hard forward."

Only half-hearing the NCO's order, Burke was already shifted back to first, and as he floored the accelerator two explosions blended into one beside the hull.

Like an animal freed from a trap, the APC bounded forward as the force of the detonation pushed the walls of armour apart, but they were taking some of the fire with them. Two of the huge centre tyres were alight and from each spun blobs of burning rubber and shreds of tread. Passage through a series of puddles failed to quench the twin blazes, the clinging mud peeling away with the softened rubber.

In a last desperate attempt Burke took the APC across the road and on to a patch of flat ground covered with a carpet of low green moss-like plants. Cascades of stinking slime and foul, brown water rose higher than the vehicle's roof as it plunged across the flood. Broken crescents of steel mesh-reinforced concrete crunched under the steaming tyres as they rode over the fragments of the bomb-shattered sewage pipe.

The raw effluent extinguished the flames but brought a torrent of obscene condemnation down on Burke as he steered them back on to the road. Much of the filth thrown up by their wild progress had found its way in, and the stink of the cordite had been replaced by another stench more powerful and more obnoxious.

Some of the mess had dripped on to Libby, but he was hardly conscious of it, only making a half-hearted move to brush it off. Sitting deep in one of the bucket seats he could see out through the open top and, high above the vision-blurring haze of the permanently suspended dust particles, he saw the interwoven contrails of the helicopter's fighter escort.

It barely registered with him, but that portion of his mind still functioning on a professional level, told him the number of escorts was just too many for a single helicopter. He would have mentioned it, but felt the battle was no longer any business of his, he was taking no more part in it.

Cline repeatedly struck the top of the radio with his clenched fist before reluctantly letting Boris remove the side panel to examine it. There were beads of bright fresh metal hanging frozen from most of the components, where solder from the circuit boards had begun to drip in the heat from the tyres immediately below the vital equipment.

"Did you get the major his air cover?" Libby wasn't really interested, just asked for something to say, to break the isolation he felt growing about him.

"I don't know. They were receiving, but I didn't get an acknowledgement." Cline entered the fact in his log, brushing aside the charcoal black ashes that spread from the edges of the small page across its neatly lined surfaces. He had to cover himself, nothing that went wrong was going to be down to him. The Russian, that was it, if there was an enquiry he'd blame it all on the enemy deserter. "What's your interest, I didn't think you cared any more, thought you were packing it in?"

For a reason he didn't understand, Libby found that funny. That was a good one, him not caring, not caring. The trouble was he cared too much; much too much. "There's no need for me to pack it in." Standing, Libby stood looking out of the gaping hole where the turret had been, feeling the wind buffet past him as their driver piled on all the speed he could. The Land-Rover was following them again, though now keeping an even more respectful distance, sometimes out of sight half a mile behind them.

Libby felt the laughter rising inside him once more, and fought it down. Him, pack it in? Oh, Cline could be so stupid, so ready to talk first and think afterwards! What need was there for him to give up, or give in? All he had to do was wait and others would do it for him. He had no need to end his battle, when the battle was about to end him.

As he saw them skimming towards the APC at zero feet, their pylons loaded with masses of lethal ordnance, he felt like throwing his arms open wide to welcome, to symbolically embrace the four Soviet Hind helicopter gunships.

Closing his eyes, Libby turned his face to the sky and waited for the obliteration of his existence. Helga was in his mind, on his lips . . .

SIXTEEN

Now they had broken from cover it no longer mattered whether or not the Soviet gunships had a hulk-discrimination capability. The APC marked itself out from all the other armoured vehicles strewn about the war-destroyed landscape by being the only one moving.

His hatch had jammed, and Revell had to leave his seat and move back down the compartment to stand and look out through the circular hole where the turret had been. He did so in time to see the helicopters close to two thousand yards and move into line astern to commence their attack run. No manoeuvre their driver could throw the clumsy vehicle through could shake them off. They had only one chance.

"Bale out and scatter."

Even before they stopped, the escape hatches were crashing open. This time it was Boris's turn to be helping someone else, as with assistance from Hyde and Andrea he pushed Libby over the side of the hull, and joined with the others in dragging the protesting man away from the personnel carrier.

From behind the inadequate protection of a curled length of T72 track, Revell could see the front seat weapons operator in the lead gunship hunched over his sights. At any second he would unleash a mass of steel and explosive towards the APC and surrounding area. He knew that by abandoning the carrier they had not avoided death, merely changed its timing and nature.

Not wanting to see their moment of firing, Revell turned his attention to the weaving contrails high overhead, and saw the silver cruciform tip of one transformed by a fireball into a smoke-towing collection of odd-shaped sections of bright metal. Another went the same way. A third Soviet aircraft tumbled from the enveloping smoke of a near miss with dark smoke billowing from its shattered cockpit as it went into a flat spin that, by the violence of the centrifugal forces it imposed, began to wrench first the control surfaces, and then the wings from the stricken aircraft.

The Soviet gunship fighter leader had released only two air to ground rockets when it ran into the solid wall of 30mm cannon shells. Caught by the converging fire from a pair of Thunderbolts, the chopper broke apart and fell out of the sky.

There was little of the second and third helicopter in line to actually reach the ground, as the effects of the pounding fire and the detonation of their ammunition and fuel loads reduced them to little more than fluttering showers of torn and semi-molten debris.

Seeing the fate of the others, the pilot of the last gunship tried to break away, but a snap burst from a high-velocity rotary action cannon sheared off its tail just forward of the rotor assembly. It came down like an autumn seed case, spinning around and around. Engulfed by flame as it crashed, none of the crew escaped.

Above the dead scene of past battles the sky was coming alive, being knotted by looping vapour trails. As the Thunderbolts swept the squad's immediate attackers out of the way, their covering fighters in turn engaged and harried the Soviet and East German escorts.

Sometimes a parachute would billow close by the smudge of smoke that marked the place where an expensive piece of sophisticated technology had succumbed to the brute result of a warhead's violent chemical reaction; more often there would be nothing to differentiate the falling bodies of the crew from the other broken parts among which they tumbled.

"What the hell have we started?" Open-mouthed, Cline watched a Mig 21 dive straight into the ground under full power, sending a geyser of flame a hundred feet above its point of impact. That dispersed instantly, and then apart from a shallow steaming crater and an old sunlight-catching shred of metal there was no sign of the aircraft or its pilot.

"Whatever, we're taking advantage of it. Round up the squad, get them aboard, we're still in with a chance."

*　　　*　　　*

The three-dimensional sky battle was becoming more complex, more destructive. Now being conducted at several quite clearly defined altitudes, its original cause was forgotten. While radar homing, TV guided and heat seeking missiles inflicted casualties at the longer ranges, where the opposing aircraft came into closer contact, heavy cannon played their part and sent their share of victims into terminal dives that ended only with devastating impact on the ground, or with the mid-air destruction of the aircraft as fuel tanks or ammunition were ignited by incendiary rounds.

Libby felt cheated, had prepared himself for death and it hadn't come. It was others, thousands of feet above him, who were finding death. As Burke sent them racing for their lines he watched the aerial combat, had counted nine planes destroyed so far, and had seen as many again break off action and dive for the security of their home bases with flaring wing tanks or damaged jet pipes or gaping holes in their fuselages.

He was aware of Revell watching him, knew the officer had not forgotten the incident at the foundry, and was adding that to what he had witnessed recently. It would be done kindly, Libby knew that, but he was going to be gently but firmly taken away.

Away from the Special Combat Group was not important, had never mattered to him much, only ever being a means to an end; but away meant a destination outside the Zone, and that he couldn't bear.

It would be a place of firm discipline and soft beds, where men who only wore uniform for appearance would tell him they understood, men who had never been in combat, and whose worst loss had been their temporary removal from the comfortable consultancies they'd enjoyed in civilian life.

For most of the others in the squad, getting out of the Zone meant rest and food and safety and sex: for the woman in the Land-Rover still doggedly following it meant something less tangible, but to them even more precious, freedom. For Libby, leaving the Zone, with the danger that his departure might be permanent, meant either the destruction of his mind or the ending of his life by his own hand.

Better he stay there dead, than live like a cabbage beyond the loose boundaries of the Zone. He let his hand stray to and rest lightly on the butt of the pistol tucked into his waistband. It was not time yet, but with the wheels eating up the road as they sped under the umbrella of the NATO air-cover towards the sanctuary of the West, he would not be leaving it a lot longer.

How strange that someone like Boris, who had been through a crisis of fear, should emerge stronger from the experience; but then the Russian had seen only a year of war, and only a few months of combat. Libby had been through two years, most of it in combat save for a couple of short spells in military hospitals with painful and unglamorous wounds, and it was as though during the whole time his experiences had been diminishing him, taking something from him so that eventually his resistance to the pressures must fail.

Hearing officer and NCO discussing their position, he knew that within the next few miles they would enter NATO-controlled territory. In the past he had accepted these short breaks, knowing that he was coming back, but without asking, without being told, he knew that this time he wouldn't be. A label would be tagged to his clothing, a diagnosis applied to his mental condition, and he would be sent back to England.

He felt the butt of the pistol warming in his grasp, and at that moment knew he wouldn't be leaving the Zone.

"They're getting close."

While the major and the sergeant scrutinised the open ground ahead from the cover of the jumbled farmyard buildings, Clarence kept watch on the approaching Russian infantry patrol.

"What do you make of them, Sergeant?" Revell passed the binoculars.

A mile away, a file of large-wheeled vehicles was moving across their front. Partially hidden by the hedge-topped sunken lane in which they travelled, it was difficult to identify them. Hyde panned ahead, and found a gap in the thick, ill-kempt growth, and waited for them to come into his field of vision. The cab of the first appeared, and he identified it immediately. "They're ours. It's a convoy of Stalwarts." He saw his observations confirmed as the line of trucks emerged into the open, the forward control, high sided six-wheelers instantly recognisable.

"Then we're almost home. Tell the women to rig a white flag on the Land-Rover, and have a couple put on ours. No point in getting blasted by our own side when we're on the last lap."

A burst of machine gun fire hit a wall close by as Ripper secured a stained and tattered rag to the twisted remains of the radio aerial. "Can we get going now, I think we've been spotted?" He dived head-first into the APC as another dozen rounds came even closer.

Hyde didn't move, he was watching the Stalwarts as they drew up in the open and their crews left the cabs to work on traversing box-like mounts in their cargo sections. At that distance it was difficult to make out ... then he saw the sides of the high mobility load carriers drop, and their crews take cover, and he knew what those contraptions were.

Smoke billowed about and almost hid the trucks as their Ranger anti-personnel mine throwers began to rapidly discharge masses of the self-arming devices. Within a minute thousands of mines had been laid in a hundred-yard-wide strip across the neglected fields.

Even before the smoke had drifted clear, the vehicle's crew had remounted and the trucks were pulling out.

"Signal the women to stay in our wheel tracks." A mortar shell punched a hole in the partially collapsed roof of the farmhouse, and Revell knew they could delay their departure no longer. A fragment of slate sliced through his sleeve and he felt warm blood trickling down his arm, and looked to see it threading from beneath his cuff and snaking over the back of his hand.

The enemy patrol was just getting the range, and several more shells fell on the farm as they pulled out, while machine gun fire raked its general area. For a few moments they would have the buildings between them and the Russians. They would have to make the most of it.

Revell kept his eyes locked on the ground where he knew the mines lay concealed in the long grass. He had seen tanks being used to deliberately clear a path through anti-personnel minefields, and had seen them suffer no worse than broken tracks, but he'd never seen a wheeled vehicle attempt it, would until now have considered it too lunatic to contemplate—but they had no choice.

Just as he thought they must have reached the danger area, there were explosions under the front wheels, and then almost immediately two more. The APC lurched on one side and Burke had to fight the steering to keep them going straight.

"That's one wheel gone." Burke's words were drowned by more explosions and the nose of the vehicle dropped, and as it hit the ground another detonation lifted it up again for a brief moment before it crashed back down. Black smoke began to come in wisps through a rent in the floor plates. "We've now got the first five-wheeled APC. Anybody got any ideas as to how we do the last thirty yards?"

It might as well have been thirty miles. Revell could see where the grass had been disturbed in a couple of places, but for the location of each mine he could see, there were ten he couldn't. They were designed to maim and cripple, if they moved from the APC, now beginning to burn, then that was what would happen to them. The Land-Rover was still intact, but that too would be going no further. Mines that could blast the wheels from a tough armoured vehicle would instantly turn the softskin into a blazing death trap.

The Russians had reached the farm and set up their guns and mortars. Although the range was extreme he could hear the bullets scything through the grass, and then a bomb landed right behind the Land-Rover.

There was nothing he could do to stop them. As more shells blasted the meadow about them, the Land-Rover surged forward, steered around the stricken carrier and bucked and lurched at speed through the grass. It had by a miracle covered perhaps half the distance to safety when the inevitable happened.

Several explosions blended together and the vehicle was lifted high into the air, spurting flame and sending bodies tumbling in every direction. Wreckage rained down and a chain-reaction rippled through the minefield. Some of the women's remains were tossed again and again, suffering worse mutilation each time.

The fire beneath the APC was gaining a hold despite the efforts of Dooley and Burke with extinguishers. Suddenly Dooley hurled the half-full extinguisher away and began to scramble about on the floor at the rear of the compartment.

"What the hell are you doing? Come on, we're making a run for it."

Ignoring the sergeant, Dooley kept raking through the piles of equipment. "It's gone, it's fucking gone. Where's my fucking pack?"

Cline looked back in, as he stood on the hull steps, taking time to choose where he'd first put his feet. "I chucked it, it was one of those that went out when we were stuck between the two wrecks. Was it important?''

The crud, he fucking knew. All that loot, if only he'd kept a bit in his pockets, spread it about a little . . . Dooley thought, and remembered. He slid down the canted floor of the hull and reached for the jammed door of the safe. Shit, he'd get the damned thing open if he had to tear it apart with his teeth. Through a gaping corner he could see a glint of yellow metal.

As he took a firm grip of the hot metal and started to pull, the interior of the APC was suddenly brilliantly lit as the flames reached the fuel tank and it began to burn in earnest. Dooley felt the heat on his back, and then suddenly there was a searing pain in his foot and he had to beat out the flames on his boot. Fire was all around him and he was forced back, feeling it scorching his face and hands.

The major was the first to reach Cline, and dragged him to the side of the field where Andrea helped fix a tourniquet above the stump of his left leg. Deeply in shock, the bombardier was attempting to make a note of his injuries in his logbook.

Apart from minor wounds caused by fragments from the stray mine Cline had stepped on, all of the others made it. Then Revell looked again, and counted. Libby was missing.

Blazing wreckage and intense mortar fire obscured the minefield, and made returning to it out of the question. He'd last seen Libby staring at the remains of one of the girls, and had thought he'd been with them when they'd run for the shelter of the sunken road.

It wasn't possible to be certain, perhaps the smoke was playing tricks with his eyes, but briefly he glimpsed what looked like the figure of a man. Unarmed, bareheaded, it was walking back towards the farm, back into the Zone.

A Canadian armoured car stopped alongside. Its commander surveyed the burning APC. "There's a field-dressing station half a mile down the road. Did all your men get out?"

The smoke thickened and Revell didn't see the figure again. "Yes, all those who wanted to."

HEADQUARTERS. AIR DEFENCE COMMAND. CENTRAL SECTOR. ZONE.

General Pakovski had heard the car pull up outside, its doors slam, and now the commotion in the outer office. He had failed, and they were coming for him. Picking up the pistol he checked that a round was chambered.

The door burst open and two KGB officers strode in. They paused, then stopped when they saw the pistol.

"You have left it too late for that."

The senior KGB man reached forward to snatch up the weapon, and died with a bullet through his forehead. The other went down with two through his heart before he'd had time to display a reaction.

It was a pity it was over. Pakovski holstered the pistol and picked up his briefcase. He had enjoyed the power and the trappings that had gone with it. Now there was only one place he could go, only one place where he might be safe. It was his turn to laugh as he stepped over the bodies.

He laughed again. In the whole of the war, he was the only man to ever go willingly into the Zone . . .

ASHES
by William W. Johnstone

OUT OF THE ASHES   (1137, $3.50)
Ben Raines hadn't looked forward to the War, but he knew
it was coming. After the balloons went up, Ben was one of
the survivors, fighting his way across the country, searching for his family, and leading a band of new pioneers attempting to bring America OUT OF THE ASHES.

FIRE IN THE ASHES   (1310, $3.50)
It's 1999 and the world as we know it no longer exists. Ben
Raines, leader of the Resistance, must regroup his rebels
and prep them for bloody guerilla war. But are they ready
to face an even fiercer foe—the human mutants threatening to overpower the world!

ANARCHY IN THE ASHES   (1387, $3.50)
Out of the smoldering nuclear wreckage of World War III,
Ben Raines has emerged as the strong leader the Resistance
needs. When Sam Hartline, the mercenary, joins forces
with an invading army of Russians, Ben and his people
raise a bloody banner of defiance to defend earth's last
bastion of freedom.

BLOOD IN THE ASHES   (1537, $3.50)
As Raines and his ragged band of followers search for land
that has escaped radiation, the insidious group known as
The Ninth Order rises up to destroy them. In a savage battle to the death, it is the fate of America itself that hangs in
the balance!

*Available wherever paperbacks are sold, or order direct from the
Publisher. Send cover price plus 50¢ per copy for mailing and
handling to Zebra Books, Dept. 1770, 475 Park Avenue South,
New York, N.Y. 10016. DO NOT SEND CASH.*

GREAT WESTERNS
by Dan Parkinson

THE SLANTED COLT   (1413, $2.25)
A tall, mysterious stranger named Kichener gave young
Benjamin Franklin Blake a gift. It was a gun, a colt pistol,
that had belonged to Ben's father. And when a cold-
blooded killer vowed to put Ben six feet under, it was a sure
thing that Ben would have to learn to use that gun—or die!

GUNPOWDER GLORY   (1448, $2.50)
Jeremy Burke, breaking a deathbed promise to his pa,
killed the lowdown Sutton boy who was the cause of his
pa's death. But when the bullets started flying, he found
there was more at stake than his own life as innocent
people were caught in the crossfire of *Gunpowder Glory*.

BLOOD ARROW   (1549, $2.50)
Randall Kerry returned to his camp to find his companion
slaughtered and scalped. With a war cry as wild as the sav-
ages', the young scout raced forward with his pistol held
high to meet them in battle.

BROTHER WOLF   (1728, $2.95)
Only two men could help Lattimer run down the sheriff's
killers—a stranger named Stillwell and an Apache who was
as deadly with a Colt as he was with a knife. One of them
would see justice done—from the muzzle of a six-gun.

CALAMITY TRAIL   (1663, $2.95)
Charles Henry Clayton fled to the west to make his fortune, get married and settle down to a peaceful life. But
the situation demanded that he strap on a six-gun and ride
toward a showdown of gunpowder and blood that would
send him galloping off to either death or glory on the . . .
Calamity Trail.